TWILIGHT AT THE GATES

A collection by **Mark Allan Gunnells**

CEMETERY GATES
MEDIA

Twilight at the Gates
Published by Cemetery Gates Media
Binghamton, New York

ISBN: 9798807061478

For more information about this book and other cemetery Gates Media publications, visit us at:

cemeterygatesmedia.com
twitter.com/cemeterygatesm
instagram.com/cemeterygatesm

Cover by Rooster Republic Press

CONTENTS

Introduction ... 5

Turn the Lights Off on the Way Out ... 7

The Haunt ... 11

Reappearing Act ... 25

The Loophole ... 33

The Shop of Lost Ideas ... 37

In the Hands of an Angry God ... 45

Bird's Nest ... 49

The House of Mundane Horrors ... 61

Campfire ... 71

Timing ... 73

In the Hands of an Indifferent God ... 83

Traveler's Rest ... 85

Future Tense ... 89

Sestina for my Nightmare Man ... 93

Strange Birds ... 95

Lost in the Wood ... 99

If Heaven is a Library ... 107

Two Boys at Summer Camp ... 109

Heresy ... 113

Sean Nichols Packs It Up ... 115

Unholy Ghost ... 123

The Road of Many Hues ... 127

Fifteen Minutes Fast ... 131

Knowledge is Power ... 133

Brick at the Stonewall ... 135

Halloween Slasher Marathon ... 137

The Alien ... 141

War On Christmas ... 143

Family Reunion ... 145

The Tooth ... 147

In a Whirlwind of Autumn Leaves ... 155

In the Zone ... 165

Story Notes ... 167

INTRODUCTION

Mark is a very good and very prolific writer. I think that is probably the most I knew about him before the autumn of 2020. A well-earned reputation and a name that seemed to be in the mix whenever anthologies were announced, a novella or novel release on the horizon that caught the eye—but a writer I'd yet to really engage with. Not quite two years later, I'd say that he is hand in glove the best representative of what it means to write Cemetery Gates style fiction.

A few of the stories in this collection came from our monthly flash fiction challenges in 2021. With every story Mark sent in, we at CGM were in complete agreement that he was one of us. His stories didn't just reflect the same influences that we set out writing in homage to i.e. *The Twilight Zone*, *Tales from the Crypt*, the *Creepshow* movies—Mark's writing is vibrant, with exciting twists and swerves that you think you can predict, but more often can't.

The thing about Mark is that his writing is of a quality that fits in with many publishers, and his style is widely appealing to readers who don't just love King and Barker, but appreciate the nuance of a quiet, well-crafted scene between two companions at the end of the world—juxtaposed with what he's capable of in his longer works (thinking of the twisted, murderous domesticity of his novella *2 B.*)

Some writers are known for their angst in creation, the struggle to put words to page. But I have this picture of Mark typing out a complete piece of flash fiction—ready for publication after one sitting—between a quiet dinner with his husband and the evening's entertainment.

Twilight at the Gates is just one thread from Mark's ever-growing tapestry of work, and this is very much a themed collection. So if you're in the mood to explore tales inspired by an author's lifetime love of *The Twilight Zone*, you're in for a treat!

Joe Sullivan, on behalf of
Brhel & Sullivan

TURN THE LIGHTS OFF
ON THE WAY OUT

February 29th. A rare day, one that only existed once every four years. Kirk didn't know if that was significant or not, but he thought it was at least noteworthy.

David walked up behind the chair and placed a hand on Kirk's shoulder. "Hey, wanna go outside?"

"What for?" Kirk asked, eyes glued to the iPad balanced on his thighs.

"To look at the stars. You know, while we still can."

Kirk finally tore his gaze from the screen and looked up at his husband. "I don't know if I want to."

"You're watching it online. What's the difference?"

"The difference is huge. Watching it on the tablet doesn't seem quite real. Like I'm watching a movie or something, and eventually the credits will roll and I can get up and return to normal life. If I go outside and see it for myself then there's no filter, no pretending. It will be *really* real, and I don't know if I can handle that."

Walking around the chair, David squatted down next to him and gently turned the iPad over on his lap. "I know you're scared. I'm scared too, but I would feel a lot better if we were scared together. I don't want to go through this alone."

Tucking the tablet aside, Kirk leaned forward and kissed David then two of them remained still with their foreheads pressed together for a moment, clasping hands like two children lost in a fairytale forest.

"What do you think is happening?" Kirk asked, his voice trembling.

David pushed up and pulled Kirk to his feet as well. "Come on, let's go do a little star-gazing. It'll be romantic."

They put on coats though the night was mild and left by the backdoor, stepping out onto the small open patio. Kirk remembered when they'd first bought the house two years ago, they had talked about how nice it would be to sit out on the patio at night and look at the stars. They'd never done it, however. It was one of those things you said because it sounded good but never quite found the time for. Like volunteering at a soup kitchen or watching *Downton Abbey*.

But if they were ever going to do it, now was the best time. Now was the *only* time.

David took a seat on one of the white deck chairs, head tilted back. "There's something kind of beautiful about it."

Kirk sat in the chair next to him, but he kept his head down, looking at his own hands. He couldn't quite bring himself to lift his eyes to the expansive night sky. "I don't know how you can say anything about this is beautiful."

Reaching across and taking Kirk's hand, David smiled at him. "The mysterious is always a bit beautiful. It's like love. No one can really explain it, no one knows exactly how it starts or ends, and that's why they write so many songs about it. The mystery of it adds to its beauty."

Kirk found himself returning his husband's smile, despite what was going on around them. Or more to the point, above them. "Suddenly you're a poet."

"I've always been a poet. Remember when I used to recite that 'beans are good for the heart' ditty?"

Kirk laughed, kissed David again, and finally felt strong enough to turn his gaze heavenward.

Something was definitely wrong, that was noticeable almost instantly, but he mused that if you didn't know what you were looking for, it may take a few minutes to pinpoint the problem. Kirk had never been into astronomy so his knowledge of constellations was a layman's minimum. He did recognize the Big Dipper, or maybe it was the Little Dipper. It was *a* Dipper nonetheless. However, some of the other constellations were obviously missing. A lot of them actually. Even as he watched, two of the stars on the Dipper's handle flared and then sputtered out, like dead bulbs.

The phenomenon had first been noticed three hours ago, stars simply winking out of existence in the sky. Scientists were baffled, and actual astronomers using their most high-powered telescopes could not figure out what had happened to these stars. Almost as if they had simply ceased to exist.

Talking heads filled the TV and internet, all offering theories and speculations, but the raw truth was that no one knew what this meant. The stars had started to disappear in more rapid succession, like a bomb's timer where the countdown sped up the closer it got to detonation. Many, even some of the talking heads, proposed that this was a precursor of the end of the world. It had been pointed out time and again that each disappearing star was the end of some world, and the earth itself was one such light in the darkness of space, and it was likely only a matter of time before we were extinguished as well.

David pointed up. "Look, I think that's Sirius blazing right there." Even before he finished the sentence, the star in question blinked out. "Or it was."

From the other side of the seven-foot-high privacy fence, Kirk heard the sound of children's laughter and he could smell the earthy smoke of the Peterson's fire pit. Mike and Sheila must be out there, letting their kids stay up late. From the sound of the children's high-pitched giggling, it seemed they didn't know anything was wrong, lost in the simple joy of getting to be up past their bedtime.

Kirk envied them.

"This isn't like the movies led me to believe it would be," he said.

David titled his head. "How do you mean?"

"In the movies, when people know the world is about to end there are riots and panic and chaos. But it's like everybody's just hunkering down and waiting."

"Well," David said, "do you feel like rioting or do you just want to be with the one you love for as long as you can?"

Kirk squeezed his hand, the only answer required.

As he stared up at the rapidly emptying sky, David said. "To answer your earlier question, I think God is closing up shop."

"What?"

"Inside you asked what I thought was happening, and that's what I think. God's had the universe open for business for a few billion years, and now he's tired, getting ready to flip the sign from OPEN to CLOSED. And what do you do on your way out? You turn off all the lights as you go."

"More of your poetry?"

"That was more of an allegory, I think."

Above them, the remaining stars began to wink out one after the other. A chain reaction, a domino effect, leaving the black sky as void as a bottomless pit.

Kirk squeezed his husband's hand again. "You were right, there's no one I would rather be here with than you."

David leaned toward him, placing a hand against Kirk's cheek. "Listen, there's something I want to tell you while there's still time. You have been–"

THE HAUNT

Only two of the five survived the fire.

***

It was Janice's idea. She'd read about the club on one of the paranormal websites she loved to scour. The paranormal was sort of her *thing*, and she fancied herself quite the expert. She'd read dozens of books, watched dozens of documentaries, interviewed people who claim to have had firsthand experiences with ghosts and demons and other otherworldly phenomenon.

Her knowledge, however, was strictly academic. She herself had never had any firsthand experiences, which had a tendency to depress her. So she was always on the lookout for purportedly haunted or cursed locations she could visit to try and touch the mystical. She never had any success.

Until The Haunt.

***

"A haunted nightclub?" Brent said then laughed. "You can't be serious."

Janice sat across from her boyfriend in the diner's cramped booth. She'd handed him the printouts then guzzled black coffee while he read over the article. She'd hoped for more enthusiasm from him and less mocking.

"Why not?" she said. "If a house can be haunted, why not a nightclub?"

"For that matter, why can't this diner be haunted? Or a department store, or a treehouse, or a doghouse?"

"Exactly."

Brent handed the papers back to her. "I was kidding, Janice."

"I'm not. Did you read the history of The Haunt?"

"Yes."

Janice gave him her patented skeptical look, right eyebrow arched and lips pursed like a little kid wanting a kiss. Brent had a habit of humoring her, which always left her in a foul humor. "So what did the article say?"

He fiddled with the salt and pepper shakers, hem-and-hawed for a bit before saying, "Something about a fire."

Janice shoved their plates out of the way and laid the papers out on the table, pointing to specific paragraphs as she spoke. "The Haunt was very popular back in the 90s and early 2000s. A lot of local bands, but it also pulled in some bigger names, usually ones on their way down but still with enough cache to pack the place. Anyway, on Halloween night, 2008, this retro-punk band called the Kinky MFs was performing and decided to add some pyrotechnics to their act. Obviously they didn't know what they were doing, because they set the club on fire. Whole place burned to the ground, and dozens of patrons died."

"What about the band?" Brent asked, the story finally catching his attention.

"Only two of the five survived the fire."

"So if the place burned to the ground...?"

"They rebuilt in 2010," Janice said, her excitement building. She was a born storyteller, and her enthusiasm for a subject that caught her interest had a way of intriguing even the most hardcore skeptic. "Right on the site of the original club. But the new Haunt only stayed open for a year before closing down for good."

"Let me guess why. Ghosts?"

"We're talking paranormal activity off the charts. Not just moving objects or shadow-figure apparitions, but actual physical manifestations, people being pushed and scratched and burned. It got so bad bands refused to play there, and business suffered so much that they had to close the doors."

Brent leaned forward and took a sip of his lukewarm coffee. "I'm not trying to shit on your cracker or anything, but I can tell you as someone who has been in more than a few bands, nightclubs come and go. Their popularity waxes and wanes. Nothing supernatural about that."

"Just look here," Janice said, pushing the papers back toward Brent. "There is actual evidence of what I'm telling you."

Brent indulged, skimming the pages. "I see newspaper articles about the fire in 2008, the deaths, some obits for the band members, the reopening and subsequent closing. I'm not doubting any of that. But as for the ghost stuff, all you've got here are some stories from folks who claim they had experiences. Judge Judy would call that hearsay."

"You're such a Scully."

"A what?"

"You know, the skeptical one from *The X-Files*."

"You know I don't watch old TV shows."

"Why do you think people would make up stories like this?" Janice asked.

Brent shrugged. "I don't know. If the club was floundering after the re-open, maybe the owners thought claiming it was haunted could get them some free publicity, drum up business from the morbid crowd."

Janice leaned back and nodded, as if Brent had just proven her point. "Now that's a consideration as well."

"What are you talking about?"

"I think the Goth-Hicks should do a show at The Haunt."

"But you said it was closed down."

"It is, but I did some digging online, found the contact information for the current owners and got in touch. They are willing to rent us the location for a night at a very reasonable rate."

Brent drummed his fingers on the table while staring down at the papers. "That would be a good angle, I have to admit. We could open the show by covering that song, 'This Club is a Haunted House.'"

"Precisely. I think we could even get a little local media coverage out of this. Really boost the band's profile."

Brent broke into a wide grin then leaned across the table and kissed Janice. "Babe, you're a genius. Let's do it."

***

The Goth-Hicks had been together for three years, performing at local clubs and venues, festivals and even Pride rallies since two of the members were gay. Their sound was a surprising blend of Goth music and bluegrass. Brent was the lead singer and lead guitarist, a natural front man with his striking but androgynous good looks and deep soulful voice. Kyle played bass guitar and Tyrone rhythm (sometimes banjo when the song called for it). They had been a couple when the band first formed then broke up then got back together then broke up again. Currently they were defining their relationship as BWB,

Buddies Who Bone. Celia was on drums, and the aggression she took out on the skins was masterful. For such a petite woman, behind her kit she turned into a beast.

Janice wasn't officially a member of the band, but they had on occasion used some of her dark poetry as lyrics. In fact, many of their most popular songs—"Nightmare Man," "Bleeding Heart," "Suicidal Love"—boasted Janice's lyrics. Plus she had a real mind for promotion and marketing.

When she and Brent presented the idea of playing The Haunt, the rest of the band went nuts for it.

"I've heard about that place," Tyrone said. "Think *Buzzfeed Unsolved* did an episode about it. The little Asian guy just about lost his shit, said he felt something tug on the back of his shirt."

Kyle paced in front of their van, his usual bundle of kinetic energy. They were in the parking lot of the Spinning Jenny, the venue they'd played that evening to a crowd of barely a dozen, not their best crowd but sadly not their worst either. "We could really parlay this into something. The paranormal scene is hot shit. There's only like a gazillion ghost hunting shows on TV and the net. We could become known as the band that serenades the dead or something like that."

"We might even get invited to play in some of the clubs in Savannah," Celia said, her drumsticks still gripped in her hands. It had been speculated she slept with them under her pillow. "I mean, the city likes to tout itself as the Ghost Capital of America or whatever. If we can get in on that action maybe one of those ghost hunting shows might want to cover our performance, we'd get on TV and gain national exposure. A recording contract couldn't be far behind that."

Celia had a way of getting carried away, her imagination taking her instantly from this small parking lot outside the Spinning Jenny to worldwide fame and astounding fortune. Her extrapolations could be infectious.

"Okay, before we embark on our world tour and pick out our mansions," Brent said, bringing them all back down to earth, "we need to work out the particulars of this gig."

"What particulars?" Tyrone asked.

Brent looked to Janice and she laid it out for the group. "It costs a thousand to rent the place for a night, and trust me that's a bargain. That means we'd each have to cough up only two hundred bucks."

Kyle stopped pacing for a minute. "Wait, you mean we wouldn't get paid for the show but would have to actually pay out of our own pockets?"

"It'll totally be worth it in the long run," Janice said.

"Absolutely," Celia agreed, which came as a bit of a surprise. She and Janice agreed on very little, both vying for the title of Alpha Chick in the group. "The publicity we get from this should give us a huge return on our investment."

Tyrone stepped next to Kyle and put a hand on his shoulder. "As long as there is actual publicity."

"I've already got a commitment from a guy at the *Greenville News* to do a story on the show," Janice said with a smug smile. "And a firm maybe from WYFF News 4. I also contacted this paranormal group out of Asheville. They have a YouTube channel called the Asheville Society of the Paranormal or A.S.P. They've agreed to come to the show and do a video for their channel which has fifty thousand subscribers."

Kyle and Tyrone exchanged a glance then nodded at the same time as if synchronized. "We're in," Kyle said, speaking for them both.

As they loaded into the van and pulled out of the lot, the conversation was excited and enthused. Tyrone admitted he didn't quite have the two hundred, but Kyle agreed to make up the difference for him. Being BWBs had its benefits.

Janice said she'd call the owners of The Haunt the following day and start making the arrangements.

***

Halloween night.

Of course. They would have been mad not to capitalize on The Haunt's history. What better night to do their show than the anniversary of the tragedy? Some might call that disrespectful or even ghoulish. Janice called it smart marketing.

As they drove to the club, Brent behind the wheel with Janice in the passenger's seat, the other three in the back of the van wedged between all the instruments and equipment, Janice did some rapid-fire texting and kept everyone up to date.

"So no word back from WYFF so that's probably a bust. However, Paul from the *News* confirmed he'll be there. And A.S.P. plans to be at the club about an hour before we open the doors at ten. They are going to stream our performance live as part of their Halloween special."

Celia reached out and struck one of the cymbals with the drumstick clutched in her left hand. "Hot diggity damn! I can feel it, can't you guys? Our big break is just around the corner."

Of the group, Celia had always been the most fame-hungry. Not that she didn't care about the music as well, but she saw it as a means to an end. A path toward recognition and money.

They pulled up to the rear entrance of the club via the narrow alleyway at seven p.m. Three hours before the start of the show, but they had to get everything unloaded and set up themselves. After backing up as close as he could get to the corrugated metal roll-up door at the back of the building, Brent hopped out and opened the van's back double doors. The band began hauling out equipment.

Celia took the key the owners had given her and let herself into the backstage area. She had been in yesterday with Brent to get the place cleaned up. They didn't go above and beyond; they didn't need the place to be spic-and-span for a rock show. They'd knocked away the worst of the cobwebs and ran a push broom across the floor. Janice also taped paper skeletons and witches to the walls, and set out a dozen jack-o-lanterns that the group had carved. "Setting the scene," she called it. The last thing they did was remove all the tables and chairs to make room for the crowd they were expecting.

A.S.P. had been teasing the performance on their YouTube channel, and Janice had posted about it on several paranormal sites. There seemed to be a buzz building that made the band feel they could draw the largest audience of their career tonight.

A few steps inside, Janice stopped abruptly. Her senses told her that something was off.

Not sight, as she hadn't turned on the light yet and it was too dark to see anything. Not smell, because the dusty scent of disuse that tickled her nostrils was no different than it had been the day before. Not touch, as she felt nothing but the cool damp air on her skin. Not taste, because all that lingered on her tongue was the Chinese takeout they'd had an hour before.

Sound. That was the sense that alerted her to something being amiss. She should have heard nothing but silence in the abandoned club, but instead she heard noise. A lot of it. Raised voices and raucous laughter and stomping feet, coming from somewhere near the front of the club.

"We're not alone," she said in a stage whisper as Brent walked in carrying an amp.

"Sounds like the tagline from some horror mov–"

His words cut off abruptly as he too heard the noise. He put the amp down and started toward the voices, Janice trailing behind him holding on to the back of his shirt. They followed the short hallway that led to the stage, and when they peaked around they were shocked to see that the main area of the club was packed. At least fifty people jostling for space in the dim lighting. The evening was strictly a BYOB event since The Haunt no longer had a liquor license, and everyone had a bottle in their hand it seemed. Outfits ranged from leather to vinyl to jeans, but the predominate color scheme was black-on-black. Hairstyles ran the gamut: Mohawks, long hair, dread-locks, lots of neon colors, even a few shaved heads.

"What the hell are they doing here so early?" Janice said. "And how'd they get in without the key? Did we forget to lock up when we left yesterday?"

At first Brent didn't respond, and when he did, his voice was tinged with awe. "Celia's right. This is going to put us on the map. If this many people are already here, we're going to be turning people away by ten."

Though surely their voices couldn't carry over the din, the crowd seemed to notice them standing there at the edge of the stage. From somewhere in the back a chant started, and soon everyone took it up so that it blasted loud as thunder.

"Mu-sic! Mu-sic! Mus-ic!"

"Holy shit!" Tyrone exclaimed, coming up behind them. "They want us, they really want us!"

Kyle was with him like a pale-skinned shadow. "Sounds like they might riot if we don't get out there."

Janice pulled out her phone and began tapping her thumbs on the screen in a rapid-fire motion.

"What are you doing?" Brent asked.

"Texting A.S.P. and Paul to see if they can get her early. I think you guys need to haul your stuff on stage as quick as possible and start the show. When you have an audience this eager, best to not keep them waiting."

***

The set started off strong. The band had never sounded better, and the crowd seemed into it. A bit of a mosh pit started near the stage, and everyone in the club gyrated and jittered as if they had an electrical current running through them. Which in a way they did. The music was the electrical current that set their nerve endings ablaze.

The band rank in the adoration, but each had their mind focused on something different.

Brent, as usual, focused solely on the music. When he was on stage, he entered his own little bubble where he became one with the rhythm, totally enclosed from the rest of the world. He could be playing for a crowd of two or two-thousand, it was all the same to him in the moment. The performance was all that mattered.

Kyle and Tyrone flanked Brent, and both the men scanned the faces nearest the stage. They had recently talked about having a threesome. In all their on-again-off-again years together, they'd never done that before. They were so high on tonight's performance, they thought that might celebrate by sharing someone. They simply had to find that someone, but surely he was out there somewhere in the crowd right now.

Behind her kit, Celia was wishing she had a better singing voice. She loved the drums, but rarely did drummers get noticed. They were always in the background, providing the driving beat that created the foundation for the band's sound but not getting the credit they deserved. If the band really did make it, she would reap the financial rewards along with everyone else, but that wasn't enough for her. She wanted her face to be known around the world.

Janice, from her vantage point out in the crowd, felt disappointment as well. Not with the show itself. No, the band was killing it and the audience was eating it up. When the Goth-Hicks performed their latest song, "Sacrifice of the Innocent," the crowd went wild, which caused a blossom of pride to bloom in Janice's chest since the lyrics were hers.

Her disappointment came from the fact that nearly an hour into the set, nothing paranormal had happened. She'd run around and lit all the stubby candles in the jack-o-lanterns which created a suitable mood, and when it became clear that neither A.S.P. or Paul were going to be able to get to the club early (Paul, in fact, had sent an apologetic text saying he might not make it at all because his youngest got sick, which reinforced Janice's intention never to have kids), she pulled out her phone and began live streaming the show from her Facebook page. Within minutes, she had about a hundred people watching, which wasn't bad.

But she'd promised people more than just a killer show. She'd promised a paranormal extravaganza and was failing to deliver. At the thirty-minute mark, she noticed the numbers on the live stream started to dip.

Where were all the fucking ghosts? With a history like The Haunt's, she expected to finally come face to face with the supernatural, a culmination of her lifelong passion, but the deformed faces of the crudely carved jack-o-lanterns were the scariest thing she'd captured so far.

She wondered if she should have reached out to some of the local psychics and mediums in the area, but despite her firm belief in the paranormal, Janice also held the firm belief that most people who made their living off claims they could deliver messages from deceased loved ones were charlatans simply trying to make a quick buck off people's grief. She'd seen little compelling evidence that they were actually channeling the dead.

Unlike Celia, Janice's primary goal here was not to make money or even to help the band. The Goth-Hicks were important to her only because they were important to Brent, but if the band broke up tomorrow and Brent got a job flipping burgers at a fast food joint, she'd be just as happy.

No, her goal here was to finally get a glimpse beyond the veil, to touch something that defied explanation, to prove the existence of life after death. Even if to no one but herself. She had been on this quest since she was twelve and saw the movie *Ghost* for the first time. She didn't think she could stomach another failure.

The phone buzzed in her hand, alerting her to a text message. She ignored it as she was in the middle of the livestream, but a few minutes later it buzzed twice more in rapid succession. Since nothing particularly interesting was happening at the moment, and the band had just started their song "Devil's Eyes" which she'd had no hand in writing, she paused the stream and checked her messages. All three were from Paul.

The first: "Kid is vomiting worse than the chick in Exorcist. Not going to make it, sorry."

The second: "I just turned on your livestream, is the band rehearsing?"

The third: "Seriously why is the band playing to an empty club? Thought you said people showed up early."

Janice frowned, confused. The club had so many patrons in it that she couldn't turn in any direction without getting a half dozen people in the shot.

"What's the joke?" she texted back. "We've got a full house."

"I should ask you what the joke is. You've been filming nothing but an empty space with some jack-o-lanterns and Halloween decorations and the band up on the stage. It's weird. Haven't you seen the comments?"

Janice in fact hadn't looked at the comments for the live stream. She found it too hard to follow them on her phone. Now she went back into Facebook and found the post, scrolling through comments which only served to confuse her more. Left her flabbergasted, in fact.

"Band sounds good but where are all the people?"

"Bad enough their playing to an empty room but they gotta memorialize it on Facebook?"

"If a band plays but no one shows up does the band even make a sound?"

"What is this, performance art? The Sound of One Hand Clapping or some shit?"

"Fuck yo they coulda at least set up some manikins or something to make it look like they had fans."

"This is sad. This is so sad."

Janice lifted her gaze from the screen and scanned the club. The crowd pressed close, bouncing and jerking to the music in a Saint Vitus dance. This was one of the biggest audiences they'd had in years, and people online were acting like there was no one here. Was it some elaborate practical joke? Maybe Brent had contacted Paul and some other friends and got them to participate in this ruse to fuck with her. Only problem with that scenario—Brent had already been on stage when she decided to do her own livestream of the show. He couldn't have known.

The nearest patron to Janice was a young guy with a bright purple Mohawk and multiple face piercings, the one in his nose connected to one in his eyebrow with a length of chain. He wore a leather vest that exposed the intricate tattoos that snaked down his arms like sleeves of ink, also spreading up his neck in a black-and-blue rash. Trembling slightly, she reached out and put a hand on his bare arm. The flesh was cold. Not just cool, but like putting her hand on a block of ice right out of the freezer. Janice gasped and pulled her hand away, causing the man to look at her with empty eyes. Pools of pure blackness staring into her soul. Janice let out a frightened gasp, her breath escaping as steam in the suddenly frigid air.

Though the band continued on, oblivious to everything but the music, Tyrone going to town on a banjo solo, Janice felt suddenly alone in an abyss devoid of sound. Every patron in the club went still, turning their dark, dead eyes on her. The temperature dropped further until she felt as if she were standing naked on an arctic tundra. Her phone slipped from numb fingers and clattered at her feet. She wanted to scream, she wanted to run, but she was frozen, immobile and mute.

On stage, Brent's gravelly voice broke in with the song's hook. *"The devil's eyes drill into me like ice. I would run but the pain feels so very nice."*

This was what she had been seeking for all these years, and she hadn't recognized it. Surrounded by the dead, she had reached out and actually touched one, and yet it wasn't the transcendent experience she'd anticipated. All she felt was fear. The deep primal fear of Neanderthals standing outside a dark cave or seeing lightning for the first time. The kind of fear that could make a person lose control of her bladder.

All her longing to experience the paranormal, she now wanted to take it back. She wished to return to a state of blissful ignorance where all this was hypothetical and part of a childlike fantasy that she clung to like a favorite security blanket. The reality was too cold, too dark, and instead of suggesting the hope of life eternal, it promised a bleak perpetuity of being trapped in a tar pit.

As Janice stared back at the man with the purple Mohawk, his skin began to blister and smoke, and before her eyes he erupted into flames. The stench of burning hair stung her nostrils, and his black eyes began to melt and ooze like oil down his face. One by one, the other patrons caught fire, reenacting their final moments. Yet despite all the flames around her, Janice felt no heat. Still just the bone-chilling cold of hopelessness.

She wondered if anyone else saw this, if only her eyes could detect the phantom fire, but the music ended abruptly in the snarl of guitars, and she heard Brent shout, "What the fuck is going on?"

Hearing his voice broke Janice's paralysis, and she bolted toward the stage, dodging between ghosts that burned like torches. None of them moved, none of them screamed, accepting their fate with inhuman calm. She clambered onto the stage and threw herself in Brent's arms. "They're dead!" she sobbed into his shoulder. "It's all the people that died in the 2008 fire."

The phantom flames had enough substance that they caught the paper decorations, real fire spreading up the walls and finally creating a heat the band could feel. Smoke began to fill the air with a haze like dirty mist.

"We have to get out of here," Celia said. She kicked off her stool and dropped her sticks, which was proof enough that the situation was serious.

No one had to be told twice. The room before them had rapidly become engulfed in flame, which now crawled along the ceiling like a living thing that could defy gravity. The five of them hurried off stage and down the short hall into the backstage area. Kyle was first at the door, and he twisted the knob repeatedly. "It won't open," he growled.

Tyrone joined him and they began pounding their shoulders against the door, but it wouldn't budge. Brent grabbed the chain to open the roll-up door, but it seemed jammed. There were no windows to break and offer escape.

Celia pushed Tyrone and Kyle aside, clawing at the door like a wild animal. "Let me out! Oh god, let me out!"

Janice could hear the crackling of the fire as it inched closer to them like a stalking beast of nightmare. Smoke leached into the room, causing her to cough and gag.

"I think I saw an ax in an old glass case when we first came in," Brent said, coughing himself. "Maybe I can break the door down."

He went off in search of the ax and Janice took over trying to pull the chain to open the roll-up door. The smoke thickened until she could barely see her friends, and she began to get lightheaded.

She heard a banging she thought might be Brent beating against the door with an ax, but in the confusion and smoke she became disoriented and wasn't sure in which direction the door lay. Behind her, flickering light suggested the fire had found its way backstage.

***

Only two of the five survived the fire.

***

Six months later the two survivors returned to The Haunt. Or the vacant lot where The Haunt had been before it burned to the ground.

Again.

"Do you think they're still in there?"

"In where?"

"The club."

"The building is gone."

"Yes, but maybe the ghost of The Haunt still exists somewhere, on some plane. I mean, if people's spirits can linger after they're gone, why not the spirit of a building?"

Neither spoke for a few minutes, standing close but not touching, staring at the scorched earth, the rubble that still hadn't been removed. Rumor was that a developer had bought the property to erect a strip-mall, but so far there was no evidence this was going to happen.

"I hope they're not here."

"You don't want to think they still exist somehow?"

"No, not like this. If they're still around then they are probably like the others, constantly reliving the end, the fire, the pain. I don't want that for them. I want to think they've moved on into the light, or even just winked out of existence altogether. That is more comforting than the alternative. Yes, I want to think they're beyond pain."

"Do you really believe that?"

"I don't know, but I'm going to keep telling myself that until I do believe it. Or at least can reasonably fool myself."

Another moment of silence.

"Okay, let's go and I don't think we should ever come back."

"Why not?"

"Because if we do, we might see them. Then we won't be able to lie to ourselves."

They squeezed each other's hands briefly before walking away. Neither looked back.

REAPPEARING ACT

You never saw me coming.

Sorry, just a little humor to lighten the mood. Don't they say you should always open with a joke? Of course, maybe that kind of humor is only funny to someone with my condition.

Although as far as I know, I'm the only person in the world with my condition. If anyone else suffers from this particular affliction, I've never seen them.

Okay, okay, enough with the invisibility jokes, I promise.

In case it isn't already clear to you, I am in fact invisible. How could such a thing happen? Astute question, and I hate to disappoint, but I have no satisfactory answer. I wasn't part of a scientific experiment gone wrong, I didn't get exposed to chemicals or radiation or alien space rays. At least, not as far as I know. I simply ... disappeared.

When exactly I can't say. I spent years isolating myself from the world, you see, finding social interaction too difficult and messy and frustrating. Other people tended to only bring pain and disappointment with them when they set up shop in your life. And unlike others my age, I embraced the technological revolution when it came. I could have my groceries delivered, work from home, chat with people online when feeling lonely and simply shut down my computer when I began to find the chatter annoying. I could stream any movie I wanted on my own TV and not have to worry about the sweaty claustrophobic press of a crowded theater.

So if I had to speculate, I would say I made myself invisible through sheer will. I tried to make the world disappear, and instead made myself disappear. It's a theory, at least. Better than any other I could come up with.

I only discovered my predicament one day when I ran out of coffee and simply could not wait to have it delivered. I decided to make the three blocks sojourn to the convenience store on the corner. On the way I passed a woman walking a poodle, and when I said hello she jerked and looked about in all directions as if unsure where my voice had come from before continuing on. Curious behavior, but I thought little of it as I found most human behavior curious.

In the store, perusing the aisles for my caffeine fix, a man bumped right into me. He was looking straight toward me but did not veer out of the way. He cried out, looked confused, then walked on with no apology. I grabbed a can of Hazelnut and took it to the counter. When the clerk finally looked up from his phone, he screamed, started reciting the Lord's Prayer, and literally ran from behind the counter and out the door into the parking lot.

I had always suspected one had to be a little mentally unstable to work in a convenience store, but this one seemed start raving mad.

Or so I thought until I realized I could see my reflection in the plate-glass window that fronted the store. More to the point, I *couldn't* see my reflection. In the glass, I could see the coffee can, seemingly floating in the air all on its own. I stepped closer, squinting my eyes, but that only made the image clearer. The coffee was there, but I wasn't. Not even my clothes.

I was invisible.

Once the initial shock wore off, which happened quicker than you might imagine, I began to realize the possibilities this opened up for me. I didn't waste any time wondering if this were a dream or perhaps I had lost my mind, the kind of stuff a character in a book would consider. No, I accepted the reality of the situation instantly and decided to make the most of it.

I left the store with my coffee without paying. Let them report the theft to the cops. It wasn't as if they would be able to identify me in a lineup. I know, I know, I promised no more invisibility jokes, but I lied. Can you get a more unreliable narrator than an invisible man?

I began going out into the world much more once I realized I was invisible to it. I could take long strolls through the surrounding neighborhoods without fear of being accosted with banal conversation from neighbors, or hit up for money by the homeless who congregated downtown. I started going to movie theaters again, making flatulence sounds to clear out a couple of rows so I could watch in comfort and relative solitude. I even visited the home of an old high school bully, threw stuff around, flipped lights on and off, slammed doors, convinced him the place was haunted by an angry spirit. His house is for sale now. Petty, I know, but deeply satisfying.

I even started visiting homes at night to take in a little live-action porn. I can tell this part makes you a little uncomfortable so I won't linger on it. Suffice to say, you'd be surprised to discover that it is often the most vanilla looking couples that have the most kinks and peccadillos.

All pretty harmless fun, really. Okay, I admit some of my antics may have had a few barbed-wires in them. For instance, I liked to go to the children's park, filled with fat spoiled brats who never heard the word "no" and thought the world owed them something just because their parents doted on them like they were little princes and princesses. I would find children playing alone and whisper in their ears, telling them their parents didn't really love them, they weren't really special. They would run away crying, the seeds of self-doubt sown.

Once, I pushed an old woman down as she crossed a busy street, inching along with her walker. I had no real reason to do so, other than I wanted to see if anyone around would help her up or simply leave her lying there. The results were half-and-half. Half the people glanced at her writhing on the pavement and kept going, the other half rushed to her aid. I felt an instant kinship with those who kept going. The Brotherhood of the Unconcerned.

Now I had always been a loner and a bit of a curmudgeon, even when I was younger, but I had never been outright sadistic and cruel. Turns out when you can do almost anything without fear of consequences or reprisals, you realize how many wicked desires you harbor that you never wanted to admit to.

Don't agree? That's only because you've never experienced the freedom I have. Anyway, I digress.

Let me assure you, it wasn't all fun and games. I still did my data entry work from home and paid the bills. Even an invisible man needs some place to live with electricity and water. However, when I wasn't at the computer, I was out terrorizing people for my own amusement.

Don't look at me that way, it wasn't as if I really hurt anyone. Not seriously, anyway. And no one got killed or anything. It was ... well, if not exactly *harmless* fun, fun that caused minimal damage.

Things continued that way for almost six months, up until the day he entered the picture.

The house across the street from my own had been vacant for almost five years. I remember looking it up on Zillow once and finding that the seller was asking way too much for a house of that size. I predicted then that it would never sell.

He proved me wrong. Either the seller finally came down on the price, or he was rolling in dough and could afford to over-spend.

I was at the computer working when I heard the moving vans pulling up, and I went to my front window to see what the commotion was all about. Two vans worth of furniture and boxes were unloaded and hauled inside, but at first I wasn't sure who the new owner-or-ers might be.

Only after the movers had finished their job and left did I get my first look at him. He came out of the house wearing only shorts and a T, walking out to the sidewalk then turning to gaze back at the place with his hands on his hips.

Love at first sight? Of course not, I don't believe in anything so prosaic and cliché. Infatuation at first sight? That I will admit to.

I had never in my life been good at relationships because they involved, you know, interacting with other people. That could quickly become tedious and boring. I had my share of one-night stands, but even those could become tedious and boring if I didn't kick them out as soon as the sex was done. Mostly I stuck to porn.

But when I got a load of my new neighbor, I felt an immediate jolt of something course through me like an electric charge. It wasn't simply that he was beautiful, which he was, but his good looks were complimented with an almost feline grace that manifested when he moved. Even his curly mop of black hair tousled elegantly, a shimmer like waves atop his head. He was more stunning than any porn star I'd ever seen on the computer screen, and I felt myself stiffening at the sight of him.

I can tell by the way you're squirming in your seat that this part makes you uncomfortable. I'm sorry, but you need to hear it. You need to hear it all, and you don't really have a choice. That's one of the perks of having a captive audience.

Anyway, as obsessions go mine started fairly low key. I began spending more time at the window, waiting for him to make an appearance. Sometimes he'd come out to mow the lawn or install shutters. When he started weeding the bush bed by the front porch, I got in a lot of good viewing time. I began to neglect work and got a few terse emails from a supervisor I'd never actually seen in person, but I found them easy to ignore. After the first couple, I stopped opening them altogether.

When the weather began to turn colder, my new neighbor spent less time outside. Therefore, I had no choice but to wander over and find my way inside his house. The place was small but cozy, with fresh paint on the walls and tasteful décor. I wandered around behind the beauty like a transparent shadow, watching him perform day-to-day tasks. Fixing meals, watching TV, reading books. I won't tell you that I sometimes watched him sleep or shower; that would make me sound like some kind of lech. I mean, I did and perhaps I am, but I won't tell you that.

I discovered his name off some mail he left lying on his coffee table. Jeremiah Kirsimagi. Even his name had a poetry to it, sounding like music in my head. I immediately found him on social media and started following him on both Twitter and Instagram. Twitter he used infrequently, but his Instagram was full of pictures detailing the renovations of his new home.

I found out from his Insta-story that he was a freelance artist who made a decent living doing book covers and movie posters, and this was his first house after living in apartments his entire life. He seemed excited, almost giddy, which made him even more adorable.

I noticed that he didn't post many pictures of himself, meaning that despite his beauty he did not feel the need to flaunt it. This indicated a lack of ego and vanity that was admirable. Made me love him even more.

Love? No, I told myself, that was ridiculous. Love was a concept in which I didn't even truly believe. My philosophy had always been that people merely got so afraid of dying alone that they would cling to the nearest person and call it love. Intellectually this made the most sense to me.

Yet I couldn't seem to shake my growing feelings for Jeremiah. I spent more and more time at his place, gazing at him in wonder. He didn't socialize much. On occasion he would go out for a drink, me trailing unseen behind him, and he'd chat with people at the bar, but he always went home alone. He was no social butterfly, our Jeremiah. A loner, like me. I felt a kinship with him which tore down my walls and eventually made me admit the burgeoning love that burned in my heart, not unlike acid reflux.

This frightened me. I know what you must be thinking. What kind of person takes becoming invisible in stride but becomes afraid by the realization that he cares for someone? Well, I guess I'm that kind of person.

I hoped the feeling would pass, again like acid reflux, but instead it only intensified and began to feel like a bubble expanding in my chest. Creating pressure and discomfort bordering on actual pain, and I needed to shrink this bubble before it burst. I decided the best way to combat this feeling would be to remove myself entirely from Jeremiah's presence. I returned home, closed all the blinds, resisting the temptation to peek out across the street. As they say, out of sight, out of mind. Ironic coming from me, I know.

However, like most old adages, that one turned out to be bullshit as well. It seemed the more I tried not to think about Jeremiah, the more he was the *only* thing I could think about. I wondered what he was doing, where he was going, what he was eating, what he was wearing. Had he decided to change brands of shampoo and I was unaware? Was he experimenting with vegetarianism?

I *needed* to know. The need manifested as a physical pain like a cramp in my gut.

After only a month, I decided to compromise. I would check in with his social media, do a little online stalking, get a glimpse into his life that way. Now I wish I hadn't done that.

Because that was when I discovered you.

Your face was all over Jeremiah's Instagram. And a beautiful face it is. Not as beautiful as Jeremiah's, but definitely worthy of the silver screen, and your skin is flawless. I could see instantly why he would have fallen for you.

And I instantly hated you for it.

From the Insta-story, I learned that you had only recently moved to town, Jeremiah had met you at the bar, the two of you had chatted for hours, you asked him out on a date, and then you became practically inseparable after that. Joined at the hip, as they say. Peas in a pod. Ying and yang.

Although never a religious man, I will admit I prayed that Jeremiah would tire of you quickly. When that didn't seem to happen, I ventured back across the street to observe the two of you in person. The first thing I noticed was how he looked at you. With such absolute devotion and delight. You made him smile and laugh more than I had seen or heard in all the time

I'd known him. You seemed to bring him out of his shell, and the two of you went out a lot. Dinner at restaurants, movies, plays, even a chamber music concert.

Jeremiah was like a new person ... and I didn't like that. I wanted him in his shell, where I could relate to him and have him all to myself. Even if he didn't know it.

My hatred for you grew. Even small things enraged me, like the fact that you called him "Jerry," taking his lyrical name and turning into something blunt and ugly. You couldn't truly appreciate him, not the way I did.

I knew I had to get rid of you, so I started my campaign. First I simply followed you when you weren't with Jeremiah, hoping to find out you were screwing around on him or had a hidden drug habit, anything that would turn him against you. But no, you visited your Mom, you volunteered at the soup kitchen downtown, and you worked as a nurse at a pediatrician's office. You gave me absolutely nothing to work with.

So I resorted to plan B. I wanted to scare you away, but I couldn't do anything too overt. If Jeremiah thought his house was haunted, he might move and I certainly didn't want that. So I had to be a little more subtle. I tugged at your clothes, I knocked a book off the shelf when you were in the bedroom alone, I pulled your hair a few times. To my delight, the ploy succeeded in that you did start to suspect some unseen entity inhabited Jeremiah's house.

To my dismay, this did not frighten you. Instead it only seemed to intrigue you, and you even convinced Jeremiah to buy a Ouija board. The two of you giggled over the board like children that night, and I watched petulantly in the corner. I thought about putting my fingers on the planchette and spelling out some nasty message, but I recognized that would only have thrilled you more. I took your disappointment when nothing happened as a minor, petty victory on my part.

On to plan C. If I had any hope of stealing Jeremiah away from you, I needed to be visible again. The old movies didn't help, because wrapping myself in bandages like a mummy seemed a silly and infeasible idea. No, I had willed myself into invisibility; I needed to will myself back to visibility.

Except I didn't know how. All I could do was *want*, concentrate with all my being on my desire to be seen by Jeremiah. Yet every trip the mirror revealed the nothingness of my being. Besides, even if I did achieve my goal, I was an old man with a receding hairline and liver spots all over my body like a child's game of connect-the-dots. How could I ever think Jeremiah would choose me over you? It seemed a hopeless endeavor.

Until I came up with plan D.

Wrapping myself in bandages might be a stupid idea, as stupid as throwing a sheet over my head and playing the part of a Halloween ghost. But the basic premise was sound. I thought about coating my entire body in makeup, but that wouldn't work. Too easily rubbed off.

No, what I needed was the real thing, something authentic that would restore me. I made my decision and that brings us back to the beginning.

You never saw me coming.

They turned the power and water off here at my house last month since I stopped paying the bills, and letters in the mail tell me they have started the foreclosure process on the property. None of that matters, because for now we still have the place to ourselves. That is why I brought you down here to the basement for a friendly little chat.

I know, I know, it doesn't seem very friendly to hit you over the head with a rock then tie you to a chair and stuff a gag in your mouth, but all's fair in love and war. Now that particular adage isn't bullshit.

I didn't have anything in my kitchen utensil drawer I thought would do the trick, so I ordered this baby online. Came yesterday. It's a filleting knife. Should make the work easier.

I'd like to tell you it won't hurt, but I'm sure it will. Love hurts, another adage with some truth to it. If there was any other way, a plan E, I would take it, but this is the only path I see for me if I hope to be with Jeremiah.

I need a new skin, and yours is flawless.

THE LOOPHOLE

Peter paused, planting the blade of the shovel in the growing mound of dirt piling up beside him. He was only halfway done, but the muscles in his arms burned and sweat drenched him as if he'd been caught out in a sour-smelling rain.

The cemetery had no lights, but the moon above shone down bright and full, blanketing everything with a frosty glow. Peter scanned the area, the sloping field with markers and monuments sprouting up like stone mushrooms, on the look-out for any movement. He detected nothing, and after another moment's rest he picked up the shovel and resumed his work.

In the distance he could hear strident sirens and panicked screams. From the west end of town, a fiery glow lit up the horizon like a bloody sunrise, smoke churning into the air. All around him was chaos and fear and mayhem, but the Mountain View Cemetery seemed to be an oasis, an island of tranquility in the middle of a turbulent sea. Ironic, actually, when he considered what was happening in the world tonight.

He had dug far enough that he needed to climb down in the hole to continue. This put him almost on eye level with the tombstone. The tombstone Peter had picked out and paid for, and the inscription he'd written himself. "Beloved Husband, Best Friend, Light Extinguished Too Soon." Nothing particularly original, but all true and heartfelt.

At the top, the name and the dates. Thomas Rhodes. January, 3 1985 – April 16, 2022. That final date not yet a month in the past. The pain still raw, the grief still fresh, then the world went and turned upside down. What Peter was doing would have seemed insane yesterday, but today the entire universe had gone insane so this seemed the sanest act he could pursue.

He paused again, wishing he'd brought some bottled water with him, but he hadn't exactly had time to pack a bag before leaving his house. *Fleeing* his house to be more accurate. The streets between Marigold Drive and the cemetery had been like a warzone, people screaming and running, cars rushing by, a pickup truck crashed against a telephone pole. A police car with the lights flashing and the driver's door hanging open sat abandoned in the middle of an intersection.

And those *things* were out like a shambling army.

Peter had dodged and darted, zigzagging his way through the bedlam as if through a maze. All he'd taken with him was the shovel from the utility building behind the house. It served as a good weapon on the six block journey to the cemetery, but now it served its true purpose.

He heard someone shouting for help nearby, just outside the cemetery. The voice sounded female and young, and Peter wanted to help. Honestly he did, but there was no help to give. He squatted down in the hole until the shouts turned to a scream, the sounds of a scuffle and a struggle, then the scream cut off abruptly. He tried to block out what came next, the wet smacking tearing noises of someone or someones enjoying a good meal with wild abandon.

Putting that out of his mind, he got back to the task at hand. He knew time was of the essence so he pushed past the soreness and the exhaustion and let the adrenaline in his system energize him enough to double his speed.

When the blade of the shovel hit something solid, Peter let out a cry. He hurriedly uncovered the coffin, tossing the shovel out of the hole and dropping to his knees, scraping away the last layer of earth with his hands. Tears cascaded down his face, dribbling off his chin and splattering on the coffin lid.

He paused, holding his breath, listening. At first he thought he imagined the sound, an auditory manifestation of his wishful thinking, but no, there was definitely movement inside the coffin. A scrambling, a scratching, and a wordless hissing verbalization.

Peter tried to open the top half of the coffin, but it wouldn't budge. He had to retrieve the shovel and use it to pry the lid loose. The top half popped open, and Peter scooted back to the far end of the hole as the lid crashed open and Thomas sat up like a puppet on a string. His bottom half was still pinned by the bottom half of the coffin lid, but his arms were free and he reached out toward Peter as if needing a hug.

The smell that hit Peter in the face was rancid, like spoiled milk and rotted vegetation. Thomas's skin was mostly intact, though his eye sockets were empty now, shadowy craters in which things seemed to squirm and move, maybe maggots. Peter didn't want to think about that.

Because even eyeless with a head full of maggots, it was still Thomas. He thought of the others out there as *things*, but this was still his husband, the love of his life. Brought back from the dead, just as all the dead in the world had been resurrected. No one knew why. Radiation, chemical warfare, the End Times promised in the Bible manifesting in an unforeseen way. All anyone knew was that it was happening, the dead were reanimated and they craved human flesh and one bite would turn you into one of them.

Thomas leaned forward, still reaching, mouth opening and closing violently enough to rattle his teeth. He could only reach so far, however, pinned the way he was in the coffin. Peter leaned forward himself, moving slowly and stretching out one of his arms until it was in range.

Thomas, even without sight, seemed to sense the closeness of Peter's flesh. Maybe he smelled it, maybe some kind of sixth sense, but his head lurched forward and he sank his teeth into the meat of the flexor muscle. The pain was intense, and when Peter jerked his arm back, the flesh tore, some of it dangling between Thomas's teeth until he gobbled it up.

Peter leaned against the dirt wall, some of it raining down on his head. He laughed despite the pain in his arm. He laughed because of it. Because of what it meant, the fulfillment of a promise.

He looked at his husband, still struggling to free himself for the coffin, and his heart filled with love. "End of the world," Peter said in a cracked voice. "Nobody I'd rather spend it with."

Thomas responded by scratching at the bottom half of the coffin and chewing the air.

"Remember our wedding, baby? Up at the top of Paris Mountain? There was that line in the vows, *until death do us part*. Made it sound so final. Well, I think we just found a loophole."

THE SHOP OF LOST IDEAS

"Where are you right now?" Scott asked, walking down the street with the cell phone pressed to his ear.

"I'm still at work," Sheryl answered.

"Oh, I thought you'd be off by now."

"I'm working late to help Kelly prepare her presentation for the Board tomorrow."

"Well, how much longer do you think you'll be?"

"At least another hour. Why?"

"I just had the most brilliant idea, and I can't wait to share it with you."

"What is it?"

"Oh no, this isn't the kind of idea you share over the phone. Can you meet me at Capri's in an hour and a half?"

"That little Italian restaurant over on Main Street?"

"That's the one."

"Scott, what's going on? Why all the mystery?"

"You'll find out when you get there. See you soon."

Scott disconnected the call and slipped the phone into his pocket. The smile on his face was a permanent fixture, and he suspected he looked like someone who was a little light in the gray matter. Not that he cared, he was too ecstatic to worry about what those he passed might think of him.

For in just a short time, he was going to propose to Sheryl, and he had a feeling she was going to be surprised but thrilled. The two had been friends for almost a decade, since college, but it had never been more than friendship, strictly platonic. Well, there was that one drunken frat party where they'd made out and he'd groped her under her shirt, but that hardly counted.

He had known for some time that Sheryl had romantic feelings for him, she had told him as much, but he had always maintained that he saw her more as a sister. And yet earlier today when he'd gotten the text from her that the new IT guy in her office had asked her out, he had been perplexed by the predominate emotion that seized him.

Jealousy.

So maybe love wasn't a sudden lightning strike like he'd always read. Maybe it was a sneaky beast that crept up on you when you weren't looking.

Perhaps a proposal might seem like an impetuous and foolish move considering that Scott had only just realized his true feelings, but on the other hand, if you looked at it in a certain way, he and Sheryl had had a ten year courtship, even if Scott hadn't recognized it as such at the time.

As Scott passed a jewelry store, he paused and stared through the window. The only thing that would keep this proposal from being perfect was the fact that he didn't have an engagement ring to give Sheryl. He would love to just walk into this store right now and buy something extravagant and beautiful for her, but the fact was that finances were tight right now and he just didn't have the cash. Hell, he was barely making his bills as it was. Luckily, Sheryl had never been a superficial or materialistic woman and he knew she wouldn't mind.

But he did, and he vowed to start saving up so that one day he could get her the kind of ring she deserved.

Checking his watch, Scott contemplated what to do to pass the time. Too early for him to go to the restaurant since Sheryl was working late, and there was no point in heading back home. So how was he going to kill the next hour and a half? He supposed he could do some browsing but he really didn't have the money to buy anything; he would need every cent for the romantic dinner he had planned at Capri's which wasn't the swankiest place in town but wasn't exactly a fast food joint either.

Scott ducked into a bookstore, perused the shelves, then moved on to an electronics shop full of gadgets he couldn't possibly afford. After that, he just strolled down Main Street, enjoying the cool autumn breeze. Multi-colored leaves scuttled along the pavement, blowing before him as if fleeing a giant intent on crushing them. Such vibrant shades of red and orange and brown and green...

Wait a minute...green? That was no leaf, that was a twenty dollar bill mixed in with the fall foliage.

Glancing around, seeing no one nearby that might have recently dropped it, Scott bent and reached for the bill, but a sudden gust sent it spiraling away, taking it down a narrow alley that ran between the public library and the police station.

Scott gave chase, feeling a bit silly. It wasn't like he was a vagrant, but he was poor enough that the promise of an extra twenty bucks was too tempting to pass up.

Every time he almost snagged the bill, it would blow a bit further away, almost as if someone were jerking it on a string. He had trailed the twenty all the way to the end of the alley when he finally stomped it under his shoe, the end sticking out flapping like a fish out of water. Scott plucked it up, stuffed it in his pocket, then looked straight ahead and frowned.

There was a little store here at the backend of the alley, the faded sign above the door reading "The Shop of Lost Ideas." But that couldn't be. Scott had lived here all his life, and the town wasn't exactly a booming metropolis. How could there be a store here he'd never heard of? Of course, he didn't think he'd ever had reason to come down this alley before so it was possible the store could have been here for years and he'd never noticed.

The windows were caked with filth, obscuring his view inside. There was no posting of the business's hours nor was there a sign indicating whether the place was open or closed, but when he tried the door it opened. Curious, he stepped inside.

The store was small and cramped, shelves everywhere, all of them laden with clear glass bottles of various shapes and sizes. All empty. As he walked further into the place, dust kicked up from his feet as if he were walking down a dirt road. He began to wonder if whatever this place was, it wasn't long abandoned and forgotten. Some relic of a ghost town.

Scott was just about to turn back for the door when a short Asian man in a T-shirt and jeans stepped out from behind one of the shelves. He made a slight bow toward Scott and said in impeccable English, "Hello there, my friend."

"Um, hi."

"I am Gui. Welcome to my shop."

Gui was of indeterminate age. One second he looked to be mid-40s, the next 80 if he was a day. A perpetual smile curled the corners of his thin lips, and he scuttled along the floor with steps so small that you would have thought his ankles were bound together.

"What is this place?" Scott asked. "Some kind of bottle shop?"

Gui laughed softly, the sound like wind chimes. "It is just what the sign says, the Shop of Lost Ideas."

"I don't get it. What does that mean?"

"Ah, my friend, allow me to explain. Do you know the feeling when something has slipped your mind, and you *know* it has slipped your mind? It's just on the tip of your brain, but try as you might you just can't grasp it and pull it back out into your consciousness. The idea is simply...*lost*. Do you know what I'm talking about?"

"Yeah, everyone has those moments."

"Exactly, and where do you think those lost ideas go?"

"They don't go anywhere, they just vanish."

"No, you are wrong. They come here, and I house them in one of my many bottles."

Scott walked over to the nearest shelf and studied the bottles there. "But there isn't anything in these."

"Quite the contrary. Each one is filled with an idea, with inspiration."

Scott didn't want to be rude, but he couldn't help but laugh. "What kind of racket are you trying to pull? You think I was born yesterday?"

"Of course you do not believe me, few do. But I can show you. Come."

Gui started across the shop, and after a brief hesitation Scott followed. It wasn't as if the old man really posed much of a threat. Probably just a harmless nutjob. Scott would humor him; this was all actually quite amusing. If it turned out Gui really believed what he was saying, Scott wasn't sure if that would make it more or less amusing.

Scott was led to the very back of the shop where a small oval-shaped mirror hung on the wall, a jumble of uncorked bottles in a pile beneath it. Gui indicated the mirror, and Scott stared at his own distorted reflection in the grimy glass. "What am I supposed to be looking at here?"

"Just wait," Gui said with another tinkling laugh then tapped a finger on the mirror. The glass suddenly quivered like the surface of a lake, causing Scott to gasp, and his reflection was replaced by the image of a black man with a scraggly beard, lying in bed and mumbling in his sleep.

"What is this, some kind of trick?"

"No, this is Emory Gerard, a writer out on the west coast. He's catching a little nap right now, just starting to drift up out of a dream, carrying with him a wonderful idea for a spy thriller. The kind of book that could catapult him onto the best seller's list and really jump-start his career. But alas, it is not to be. He is fading back into sleep, and the idea is dissipating, unraveling into fragments that are coming…to me."

The mirror suddenly began to glow, a frosty phosphorescence that was almost painful to look at. Gui bent, retrieved a fat bottle that tapered to a slender neck and held it up toward the mirror. The light seemed to funnel into the bottle where it glowed for a moment before fading. Gui took a cork and stuck it into the bottle's opening.

"And here we are, another idea to add to my collection."

Scott bolted forward and grabbed the mirror, yanking it off the wall and looking at its back. Surely it must be some kind of disguised television or computer monitor, but there were no wires or cables, nothing out of the ordinary at all. Just a mirror, and yet…

"This is amazing. And what do you do with all these ideas?"

"Well, I initially hold them for a certain amount of time, just in case the owners retrieve them. It is rare, but it does happen from time to time. After a while, I put them up for sale."

"All these bottles are filled with lost ideas like Mr. Gerard's?"

"Not just like his." Gui walked over to one of the shelves and pointed to an old wine bottle minus the label. "For instance, this was a woman's mental reminder to take her birth control pills. Her baby boy is six months old now. And here…" He now indicated a mason jar. "This was a man's thought that he needed to get his brakes checked. Unfortunately, there is now no chance he'll ever be reclaiming this idea."

The wheels were suddenly turning in Scott's mind, and he was having an idea of his own. "Do you have ideas for get rich schemes, things like that?"

"Of course, but I feel I should make clear that all I sell here are lost ideas, untested and unproven. Just because you take the idea for a get rich scheme doesn't mean it will actually work."

"That's true." Scott thought it over for a moment then looked at the bottle in Gui's hands. He had never wanted to be a writer, but the idea of having a bestselling spy novel was certainly appealing. Could lead to an even more lucrative movie deal, and then there would be nothing he couldn't buy Sheryl.

Apparently sensing Scott's thoughts, Gui shook his head. "Sorry, this one is not for sale yet. It is still on hold in case the owner retrieves it. However, I do have something else you might be interested in."

Eagerly, Scott followed Gui to another shelf. The bottle he selected was thin and long, almost like an oversized test tube with a flat base. It was rather dusty. "This was an idea for a mummy novel Stephen King had as a young man. Unfortunately he was drinking heavily in those years as well as developing a serious cocaine habit, and he lost the idea in the fog."

"A Stephen King novel?" Scott said breathlessly.

"Well, not exactly. It's only the idea for a *potential* Stephen King novel."

"People love his stuff." Scott reached into his pocket and pulled out the crumpled twenty that had led him here. It seemed quite paltry all of a sudden. "Um, how much would you charge for something like that?"

"No money here," Gui said, waving away the cash. "This is more a barter economy in my shop. All I ask is a fair trade."

"What do you mean?"

"An idea for an idea."

Scott took an involuntary step back. "What kind of idea?"

"I would simply take one at random. Don't worry, it wouldn't be anything major like your memory of how to drive a car, or the idea that you need to check both ways before crossing the street. Nothing that could lead to any physical harm or alter the very essence of your personality."

"Would it hurt?"

"Oh no, not at all."

Scott hesitated just a moment before taking a deep breath and saying, "Okay, I'll take it."

***

Scott spotted Sheryl as soon as she stepped into the restaurant. He waved her over to the table, where two glasses of white wine were waiting. "I took the liberty of ordering the vegetarian lasagna for you."

Sheryl smiled. "You know me so well."

"That I do."

"So what's the occasion?"

"Sheryl, I just have to tell you. I've had the most wonderful idea for a novel."

"A novel?" she said with a frown, taking a sip of her wine. "You mean, like to *read*?"

"No, to write. It just came to me. See, there would be this mummy exhibit touring the country at different museums, a mother and child mummified together. Someone breaks in and steals the child. This awakens the mother and she goes on a rampage searching for her child."

Sheryl just looked at him with a bemused expression. "Scott, what are you talking about? Since when did you want to be a writer?"

"I just think this could be huge, maybe even the start of a series. You know, the next *Twilight* or something."

"No offense, but I'm going to go with 'or something.' Is that the big idea you wanted to share with me?"

"Um, no. I don't think so. There was something else...I just can't...it seems to have slipped my mind."

"Slipped your mind? You seemed awfully amped up about it on the phone earlier."

"I know, funniest thing, but I can't remember what it was. Oh well, if it was important, I'm sure it will come back to me. So, tell me about this hot date you have lined up."

IN THE HANDS OF AN ANGRY GOD

Kevin trudged from the barn back to the small cabin. The flickering firelight in the window acted as a beacon, calling him home. The snow came up to his waist so he basically had to tunnel his way through, making the relatively short journey from barn to cabin take so much longer. During the worst blizzards, the snow would freeze so solidly that he could walk on top of the crust without ever breaking through. Of course, visibility was so bad that he dared not go out when the snow was actively falling. If tunneling through the snow was the price he had to pay for a clear sky, he was willing to pay it.

As he neared the front door and the relative warmth of inside, he glanced uneasily at the sky. Still clear. It had been clear for nearly a week now. The longest streak without snow for longer than he could remember.

Not that good weather solved all his problems.

When he finally reached the cabin, he climbed the steps onto the porch, his legs feeling numb from cold. He opened the door just a crack, enough to slip his emaciated frame through, and then hurried inside and slammed the door behind him, not wanting any more heat to escape the house than necessary.

The temperature inside was cold but not frigid; at least he couldn't see his breath puffing out in front of him. Across the one room of the cabin, his wife Julia huddled in front of the fireplace, small flames licking up in the hearth. She held herself, her worn wool shawl pulled tight around her shoulders.

She looked at Kevin and the basket in his hands. "Where's the bucket?"

"I'm sorry, there will be no more milk. And these," he said, holding up the basket, "will be the last of the eggs as well."

"The cow and *all* the chickens?"

"I'm afraid so," he said, setting the basket with the three measly eggs on the floor. "I'm surprised they lasted this long. I haven't been able to properly repair the barn, and with all the cracks and holes in the wood, the cold was too much for the poor animals."

Julia closed her eyes and released a shuddering breath. "It's okay. We'll be okay. We can melt snow for water, and there is plenty enough of that. For food, we have the chickens and the cows. If they can't provide for us one way, they can provide for us another."

Kevin was struck anew by his wife's unfailing ability to look on the bright side. Once that optimism inspired a surge of love in him, but now he only felt annoyance. Optimism in the face of harsh reality was not admirable; it was delusional.

"I fear we will soon join the cow and chickens," he said. "When the next quake and blizzard come–"

"We haven't experienced those in days, love. Perhaps that ordeal is finally over."

"We've thought that before, remember?"

"Yes, but we've never gone this long without the earth shaking and the snow swirling down. I believe God may have finally answered our prayers."

Kevin didn't bother to mention he hadn't prayed in nearly a year. Instead, he said, "Even if the quakes and blizzards have stopped, it's still freezing out there and we are nearly out of fuel for the fire."

They both looked around at the empty inside of the cabin. They had broken up almost all the furniture to feed the fire. The table and chairs, the bedframe, the bookcases. Eventually even the books had become food for the flames. All that remained were two footstools, but they would provide little substance for the hungry heat.

"The barn!" Julia said suddenly, brightening. Her shawl slipped, revealing her thin neck and painfully exposed collarbones. "Since we no longer need it to house the animals, we can chop it up. Plenty of wood there."

"Much of that wood is saturated by the snow."

"So we start right away and start bringing it in to dry out. Perfect solution. See, you should never doubt God. He always provides."

"Stop saying that!" Kevin screamed and kicked out at the basket. One of the eggs tumbled over the side and cracked against the floor, yellow yoke oozing out. Not that it mattered. One egg wouldn't save them. Nothing could save them, only delay the inevitable.

Julia pulled the shawl tighter around herself, her expression setting stern like stone. "Do not blaspheme in front of me again. I won't hear it."

"The God you keep praying to for salvation, He is the one we need saving *from*. You believe He controls all that happens in this godforsaken arctic world, don't you?"

She looked away from her husband, back toward the fire. Kevin crossed the floor in long strides, grabbed Julia by the shoulders and spun her around. "Answer me, woman! Do you believe God controls all that happens in this world?"

"Y-yes," she stammered. "Of course."

"Then *He* is responsible for the quakes and blizzards; *He* is responsible for the snow never melting; *He* is responsible for the death of our animals. Every single miserable thing that has happened, He is the one who has caused it. The Master of Suffering and Despair. If He offers up temporary but inadequate solutions, it seems only to prolong our pain for His own mysterious and perverse pleasure."

Julia broke free and covered her ears, shaking her head. "You mustn't say such things."

"Why not? They are true statements. If God really wanted to help us, He would bring out the sun. Melt the snow. End this endless winter. Allow us to grow crops, properly tend animals, find others and make a community. Instead he keeps us prisoners in this icy hell, desperate and barely surviving."

Julia looked as if she were about to protest further but then the ground began to shake. Julia cried out in surprise, but Kevin could not claim any surprise himself. Yes, it had been nearly a week and he had dared to hope, but he had always known deep down that God wasn't done torturing them.

The world seemed to turn topsy-turvy, the entire world shaking and rumbling. The basket skittered across the floor and into the fire, destroying the remaining two eggs. Kevin and his wife both fell to the floor, clinging to one another.

When the quaking finally ceased, Kevin got unsteadily to his feet and stumbled to the window. Snow fell so heavily it was like a thick blanket, making it impossible even to see the barn. Always the same, the quake followed by the blizzard.

"This is your fault," Julia hissed, still on her hands and knees. "God heard what you said, and this is His punishment."

Kevin continued to stare out the window. "Blame me if you will, but I know who is truly to blame."

Suddenly he bolted to the front door, tearing it open and running out into the blizzard, dropping to his knees in the cold snow. He tilted his head back so that the deluge of freezing flakes hit him in the face. "Damn you!" he screamed at the sky. "Goddamn you God!"

***

Eddie stared into the rounded plastic globe, watching the little white flakes swirl around, almost obscuring the tiny cabin and barn figurines inside.

His mother walked into the room and smiled. "Oh, I see you finally found your snow globe. Where was it?"

The six-year-old smiled up at his mother. "Under my bed."

"Well, it's a wonder you can locate anything in this pigsty you call a bedroom. Anyway, I'm glad you found it. I know how much you love it."

Eddie looked back at the snow globe, and as the white flakes began to settle, he gave it another vigorous shake.

BIRD'S NEST

"You should let me trim that bird's nest of yours," Trish said when her husband walked into the living room. Vic plopped down on the sofa, snatched up the remote from the coffee table, and changed the channel on the TV without a word.

Trish made a swipe for the remote, but Vic held it away from her. "I was watching that, jerk."

Vic shrugged, never taking his eyes off the old Western now playing on the screen. "You're the one who likes to read so much. Go stick your nose in a book."

Trish thought about arguing, but then she reached up and touched the fading bruise on her cheek. A reminder of what arguing got her these days. With a huff, she stalked off to the bedroom, slamming the door behind her. A small show of defiance.

Which she instantly regretted, and she tensed and waited to see if he would storm after her. Instead, he merely turned up the volume on the movie.

Stretching out on the bed, Trish put a hand over her eyes and wished for the hundred-millionth time that this damn pandemic would go away to give her a little breathing room again. Vic had been out of work due for nearly nine months now, a gestation period that instead of producing a baby only produced discontent and frustration and anger.

They'd been trapped inside this house together for all that time, constantly in each other's way, getting on each other's nerves, and Trish thought she finally understood the phrase, *familiarity breeds contempt.*

Not that their marriage had been a fairytale or even particularly happy before the pandemic, but at least when Vic had been working, there had been enough time apart to make Trish's life bearable.

And Vic's temper, which had always been volatile, had really slipped the leash these past few months. And *slipped the leash* seemed like an apt metaphor as she sometimes thought of her husband as a rabid dog, snarling and foaming and ready to tear her apart just like that Saint Bernard in that old Stephen King movie. The bruise on her cheek attested to that. As well as the one on her right thigh, and on her back.

You need to leave his sorry ass, she thought. She'd been thinking the same thing for over a year now. But where could she go? She had no family except some distant cousins who were just names she sent generic Happy Birthday messages to on Facebook, and no real friends to speak of. She had no money of her own. Shortly after she and Vic got married, he convinced her to quit working because he made enough to support them both. At the time, the offer had seemed romantic and some old-fashioned part of her no doubt influenced by her own late mother had found the notion appealing.

Of course, now she saw it for what it was. A means to control her, to keep her dependent on him. A power move, plain and simple.

With a sigh, she climbed back off the bed and walked over to one of the many bookshelves that filled the house. Her love of books was the one indulgence Vic allowed her, mostly because she bought secondhand and the cost was minimal. She went through phases with her reading. For several months, she'd read nothing but espionage thrillers then switch to nonfiction books about World War II before spending a chunk of time on cozy mysteries. Her latest obsession was books about the occult, Wicca, and the history of witchcraft.

From a shelf, she plucked her newest acquisition, delivered by Amazon only yesterday. A tattered and yellowed paperback, the faded cover sporting an image of a crude figure with a spiral in its stomach holding a sun above its head, flanked by two crescent moons. The name of the book was *Spells of the Natural World*.

Trish settled into the chair in the corner, tucking her feet beneath her, and opened the book.

***

Trish waited until the Western was over and Vic turned the TV off. Then she came out of the bedroom carrying a towel, scissors, and the electric clippers. "Okay, wild man, let's cut that mane."

Vic looked over and gave her a rare smile, running his hands threw his dark locks. He hadn't gotten a haircut since before he got furloughed, and his hair now fell to his shoulders in tangled strands that curled slightly at the ends. "What, you don't like my Farrah look?"

She laughed. "Seriously, you're starting to look like someone from that zombie show."

"That's what it feels like sometimes," he grumbled but then the smile returned. "Besides, I thought all the women were hot for that dirty guy with the crossbow."

In that little teasing smile, Trish caught a glimpse of the man she'd fallen in love with. Back before she'd realized what a domineering asshole he was, before she'd got a full taste of his dark side. She thought about her bruises, and the ones that had come before, and banished all sentimentality from her mind. Sure, Frankenstein's monster had taken the flower from the little girl, but he'd also thrown that girl's lifeless body into the river.

Trish shrugged as if it didn't matter to her. "Well, if you don't want me to trim you up..."

"Hell no," he said, getting up from the sofa. "This mop is hot as hell and is always getting in my eyes."

"Great. Let's do it out in the backyard so we don't get hair all in the house."

As Vic walked past, he swatted her on the ass. "Make me look pretty like you used to."

Out in the narrow backyard, shielded by the seven-foot-high privacy fence, Vic sat in one of the aqua deck chairs that they rarely used. Trish draped the towel around his shoulders like a cape and ran her fingers through his hair, ignoring the greasy texture. "How short do you want it?" she asked in a detached, professional tone.

Vic's shoulders shrugged beneath the towel. "Don't care, as long as you don't scalp me."

Trish started with the scissors first, thinning out the thick tresses. She started slowly, a bit rusty, but soon her hands fell back into that old familiar rhythm and moved almost of their own accord. By the time she put one of the guards on the electric clippers and took them to the back of her husband's head, it was as if she had never stopped cutting hair.

In truth, it had been nearly three years. Her life as a beautician seemed so distant, back when she'd had a life of her own, money of her own, and had not mastered the art of covering fresh bruises with makeup. She'd only been working at a Great Clips inside a Walmart, but she'd enjoyed the job. That was how she met Vic, in fact, when he came in for a trim.

He flirted with her the whole time and left her a huge tip and his phone number.

Now she wished she'd thrown it away. Hindsight is 20/20 and all that.

"That feels good, babe," Vic mumbled as she ran the clippers along his head. He sounded lulled, drowsy, and she looked down as big clumps of hair fell to the ground. His hair was so thick, and a deep black that almost reflected blue in the light, that the accumulating clumps looked like some fuzzy animal about to scurry away.

It took her only fifteen minutes, and after tidying up around his ears, she stepped back and said, "All done."

He stood, shaking out the towel so that more hair tumbled to the ground. "Feel ten pounds lighter."

"You look a lot better."

He started for the house, but as he came even with her, he stopped and gave her a stern look. "I'm going to check myself out in the mirror. If you fucked my head up, I'm going to fuck you up."

There was the Vic she knew and loathed.

She stayed in the backyard for a moment more, enjoying the feel of the sun on her skin. Even though it was technically winter, the southern air was mild and almost warm. Finally she headed for the back door, whistling a little discordant tune. She heard it answered and turned to see a small red cardinal alight on the back of the deck chair and then fluttered down to the ground.

***

At noon the next day, Trish went into the bedroom and opened the curtains so that big gold bars of sunlight came tumbling in. "Wake up, sleepyhead. I made turkey pot pies for lunch."

Vic growled, rolled over to put his back to her, and buried his head under a pillow. "Turn off the goddamn light!"

"That's the sun. You'll have to talk to God about turning that out."

"Then close the curtains, you cunt."

Trish did as he asked then sat down on the edge of the mattress. "What's wrong? You only had three beers last night so you can't be hung over."

His voice muffled through the pillow he pressed on top of his head as if trying to smother himself, he said, "I have a splitting headache. Worse one I've ever had in my life."

"Want me to get you some Advil?"

"It'd take a bottle to even make a dent in this pain. I feel like there's a whole person inside my head trying to bash his way out through my skull."

"How mythological," she said with a soft laugh.

"Bitch, leave me alone!" Vic shouted then his entire frame tensed in a full-body wince. When he spoke again, his voice was quiet and plaintive. "Please, just go."

Again, Trish did as he asked, shutting the bedroom door behind her.

Vic remained in bed most of the day.

***

The following morning, Trish awoke to find Vic's side of the bed empty. After a quick trip to the bathroom, she found her husband in the living room, staring out one of the sidelights at the front door.

"Feeling better?" she asked.

He shushed her without tearing his eyes away from the glass.

She walked up behind him, gazing over his shoulder. "What are we looking at?"

"Buddy's out there cleaning his gutters."

Vic was right. Their neighbor from across the street was up on a ladder, pulling wet wads of autumn's leaves out of the gutter. "Yeah, so?"

He gave her a look as if she had just asked a stupid question like *what color is the sky?* "So you think Buddy Henderson just decided to get up at seven o'clock on a Saturday morning to clean out his gutters?"

"Obviously he did."

Vic shook his head. "Bullshit. Cleaning the gutters is nothing more than a cover."

"For what?"

"To keep an eye on us, of course. He's spying on us."

A laugh sputtered out of her mouth before she could stop it, and Vic whirled around and backhanded Trish across her already-bruised cheek. She didn't cry (she had learned crying only made him angrier); she gritted my teeth, took a deep breath, and refused to react. "So why would he be spying on us?"

He gave her another of those incredulous *what-color-is-the-sky* looks. "Isn't it obvious? He's got that Biden/Harris bumper sticker on the back of his car. I've even heard him listening to The Dixie Chicks."

"I think they go by just The Chicks now."

"My point exactly!" Vic said, his voice rising in volume and vehemence. "Buddy is clearly a communist."

She wanted to laugh again but held it in. The stinging in her cheek made it pretty easy to do. "I'll play along. Let's say you're right and Buddy is a communist. Why would he be spying on *us*? We're nobody."

"We're good upstanding patriotic Americans, is what we are. The damn commies have already succeeding in stealing the election, but they know that the real patriots know they did it, so they need to keep tabs on us, make sure we're not planning to expose them."

She nodded, trying to keep any traces of sarcasm from her voice when she said, "And that's why Buddy is out cleaning his gutters this morning?"

"Precisely. Now you're getting it."

Vic turned back to the sidelight, and Trish left him to his surveillance to make herself a bowl of oatmeal.

***

Trish walked into the bathroom to find Vic, fully clothed and sitting in the empty tub, rubbing furiously at his temples.

"Another headache?" she asked, sitting on the closed toilet lid.

He nodded, tears leaking from the corners of his squinted eyes. Trish almost felt sorry for him.

Almost.

"Maybe you should go see a doctor."

"No doctors," he said. "They can't be trusted. Might be in on it too."

"So now all doctors could be communists?"

"Anybody too educated. You say education, I say indoctrination. It's how they get our young people and we end up with an entire generation of PC-Nazis and socialists."

"Nazis, socialists, or communists? They aren't the same thing, you know."

Vic flapped a hand at Trish. "If you aren't going to be helpful, leave me alone. I need to figure out how to stop Buddy."

"What's Buddy got to do with your headaches?"

"He's causing them, obviously."

"Let me guess, he put a chip in you or something."

"Nah, I've never gotten a flu shot," Vic said as if that made perfect sense. "I think he's shooting some kind of frequency over this way and that's causing my headaches."

"But I'm fine."

For a moment, this seemed to throw a wrench in Vic's delusion and it looked as if some sense might get through to him, but then he shook his head. "The frequency must be calibrated for my specific brain waves. Probably to a man's brainwaves because they'll want to take out the men first. Women are more easily manipulated without a strong man there to guide them."

"Of course, dear," she said, standing.

Vic sank his head down until it rested against his bent knees. "Shut the curtain."

She pulled the shower curtain across the bar, sealing her husband in his porcelain deprivation tank.

***

"What are you doing out here?"

Trish turned at the harsh rasp of her husband's voice. It was mid-day, the air cold but refreshing, her breathing puffing out in a ghostly vapor when she answered. "Just doing a little bird-watching."

"What?"

She looked back up into the pecan tree at the edge of the backyard, some of the branches hanging over the fence that separated their property from the Jorgenson's behind them. She pointed at one of the lowest branches. "See, a cardinal has built a little next there."

Vic stormed across the lawn, grabbed Trish by the arm, and roughly dragged her back to the house and inside. She jerked loose of him in the kitchen, rubbing at her arm. "What's the matter with you?"

"What's the matter with *me*? What's the matter with *you*? Prancing around out there for all those commie eyes to see."

"I don't even think Buddy is home right now."

"No, but Michael is."

"Michael Jorgenson?" Trish said. "You think he's a Russian spy too?"

Vic slapped a hand down on the counter, causing the salt and pepper shakers to tremble. "They're all in on it, don't you get that? We're surrounded."

"Michael Jorgenson isn't some liberal like Buddy. Have you seen all those NRA stickers on his truck, including the one that says 'SUCK MY GLOCK'?"

"Cover, so we wouldn't suspect. I'm too smart for him though."

Trish stared at her husband for a moment before saying, "Maybe you should go see someone."

"I told you I don't need any damn doctor."

"I was thinking more along the lines of a psychiatrist."

He backhanded her again, but to be honest, it lacked his usual force. "Thank God I'm here to protect you, Trish. You'd be lost without me."

She watched as he grabbed the tinfoil out of the cabinet and pushed through the swinging door. This morning he'd been babbling about building some kind of helmet to block the headache-inducing frequencies being sent by Buddy Henderson, or possibly Michael Jorgenson, so she suspected the tinfoil would be a key building block.

After a few more minutes, when she was sure he was engrossed in his work, Trish slipped back outside and looked up at the pecan tree as the little cardinal alighted into its newly made nest.

***

Trish was in the bathroom when she heard the doorbell followed by the heavy clomping of Vic running through the house. Then came shouting and profanity. She finished her business as quickly as she could and hurried to the living room. Her husband stood in the doorway, yelling, his face turned an alarming shade of beet-red and spittle flying from his mouth. Outside, paper grocery bags huddled together on the stoop as if afraid, one of them turned on its side and spilling out oranges.

A car was parked at the curb, and a young man with a blue facemask covering the lower part of his features backed slowly toward the car, his hands held out in a placating gesture. As Trish watched in stunned silence, Vic bent and plucked a can of chickpeas from one of the bags and tossed it at the kid. The heavy can struck the boy in the thigh and he cried out.

"Vic, what the hell are you doing?" Trish said, rushing over and grabbing his arm as he reached down for more ammunition.

Outside the kid screamed, "Dude, you're nuts! I'm going to tell my boss!" Then he jumped in the car and peeled off down Belmont Avenue. Trish saw the curtains in Buddy's house across the street twitch, no doubt our neighbor getting a front row seat to the show.

Vic kicked one of the bags, brown eggs exploding out and cracking all over the walkway. Then he slammed and locked the door. "The Russian bastards are getting bold, walking right up to the door and ringing the door to say howdy."

"That wasn't a Russian. That was the delivery guy from Aldi. You know I've been having our groceries delivered, though I have a feeling we're going to be banned from Aldi for life after your little hissy fit. You could have really hurt that boy."

"They really have you brainwashed, don't they? That wasn't some boy, that was a deep-infiltration operative. That food out there is probably poisoned."

"So you want to leave a hundred and fifty dollars' worth of groceries out on the front stoop to rot? You're losing it, Vic."

He looked like he wanted to hit her but instead he pushed past, growling, "For the first time in my life, I'm seeing things perfectly clear. I may be the last sane person in this country."

After he stormed off down the hall, Trish stared through the sidelights at the groceries. As if reading her mind, Vic called from the back of the house, "Don't even think about bringing any of that tainted food into the house unless you want to lose a few teeth."

With a sigh and a shrug, Trish headed for the kitchen to see what she could scrounge up from the nearly-bare cabinets for dinner.

***

The following Sunday, Vic ripped the pages out of almost all of Trish's books.

She found him in the bedroom, huddled in the corner, surrounded by torn pages like feathers after some horrible bird apocalypse. His hands were buried in his hair and he was crying.

Crying. She had never seen her husband cry before, not even when his father died last spring.

She stood over him, hands on her hips, surveying the damage. "Let me guess, the books are communist spies as well?"

"Propaganda," he said in between sobs. "It's all just propaganda clouding your mind so you can't see the truth."

She reached down and picked up a ruined paperback. "Joshilyn Jackson is propaganda? For what exactly? Eccentric relatives?"

He shook his head, tears dripping and hanging off his chin like icicles. "I can't think. My head hurts too much for me to think. I need to make them stop. Whatever it takes, I have to make them stop."

Trish tossed the paperback at her husband. It bounced off his shoulder then landed on the carpet. "I'm not cleaning up this mess," she said and left him alone with the destruction he'd wrought.

***

A loud *BOOM!* startled Trish awake. At first she thought it was thunder, but no lightning flashed outside the windows and no further thunder followed. However, she did hear voices raised in panic somewhere outside. Vic's side of the bed was empty again, and a sense of catastrophe hit her with the force of a premonition.

Throwing off the covers, she clambered out of bed and headed for the living room, not even pausing to put on her slippers. The front door was standing wide open to the night, and Trish went running outside. The grocery bags had not been moved, though it looked as if squirrels or raccoons had gotten into them. She ignored this, following the panicked voices around the side of the house.

From the other side of the privacy fence, the Jorgenson property. That's where all the commotion originated. She backtracked to the street and went around the fence, cutting between her property and the empty house for sale next door. In the dark, she saw a shape running toward her, and she and Betty Jorgenson nearly collided.

"Oh, Trisha, I was just coming to find you."

"What's going on?" Trisha asked, nearly out of breath.

"Your husband … he was banging on our door, woke us up. My husband grabbed his gun, not knowing who it was. When he opened the door, Victor started yelling about Russian spies and communist plots. He wasn't making any sense. Mike tried to calm him down, but Trish, oh God Victor had a knife and he slashed at Mike, got him in the arm. Mike wouldn't have done it if he'd had a choice, I swear. I've already called 911 and an ambulance is on its way."

Trish pushed past Betty and continued on, tearing through the Jorgenson's backyard and around the side of the house to the front. Michael was pacing around the lawn, shirtless and wearing only boxer shorts, a dazed look in his eyes. He cradled his left arm, which had a nasty gash in it, blood gushing out to splatter the grass. He saw Trish but his eyes didn't really focus on her. "I'm sorry," he said in an almost robotic way. "I didn't want to do it, but I had to. He was out of control."

Trish noticed the Jorgenson's front door was also open, and she stepped up to it. In the foyer, Vic lay on his back. A crater was opened in his chest, and blood pooled beneath him, looking almost black, like a black hole opening in the floor to swallow him up. The butcher knife that came from the block in their kitchen was still gripped loosely in his hand. His eyes were opened and turned back toward her, but she could tell instantly they saw nothing. They were as empty as the vacant house next to theirs.

As the sound of sirens drifted to her, distant but getting closer, Trish covered her face with her hands and wept.

***

Trish walked outside, taking a moment on the stoop to breath in the fresh air. Spring was just around the corner, and she could feel it on the breeze that brushed her face. She glanced at the FOR SALE sign planted in the front lawn. Her real estate agent said they had a serious offer on the table, so as long as there were no delays with the couple getting the loan they should be able to schedule the closing by the end of the month.

She walked around the house to the back, planning to read in the sunshine. In her hands, she held her copy of *Spells of the Natural World*. One of the few books that had escaped Vic's wrath. This one had been safe though because she'd kept it tucked under the mattress on her side of the bed.

In the backyard, she paused again to make sure she didn't hear the Jorgenson's on the other side of the fence. She couldn't take any more of their guilt and apologies. Michael in particular was taking it hard, and Betty had told Trish that he got rid of all his guns and denounced his membership in the NRA. She supposed some men liked to play at being a cowboy but didn't have the actual guts when faced with the reality. In any case, she had assured them time and again that she didn't blame them.

Though she would never say it out loud, she actually felt grateful to them.

Looking at the back of the house, she thought about how much she wouldn't miss this place when she was gone. Held too many bad memories. The money she got from the sale coupled with what was left of Vic's life insurance after the cremation expenses should get her set up in a little apartment and keep her comfortable while she looked for a job. There were plenty of salons in town, so even with her having been out of the game for a while, she felt confident she'd find something before too long.

A light twittering caught her attention, and she looked up at the lowest branch in the pecan tree. The cardinal was in its nest, seemingly singing to her. She whistled to it then said, "Thank you, my friend. You have played your part, and now I discharge you from service."

With a final tweet, the bird took flight and soared up and over the house. Trish watched it go then turned her gaze back to its nest. A smile curled her lips as she admired the structure's simple but intricate architecture, woven from twigs and grass and several deep black strands that almost reflected blue in the light.

THE HOUSE OF MUNDANE HORRORS

There were five of them crammed into the compact car. Frank was driving with Mimi by his side. Drake, Ralphie, and Al jostled for room in the backseat. One of them could have easily fit in the front, but Frank liked having Mimi all to himself. He smiled over at her, and he thought he sensed a smile in return, but it was hard to tell with dirty bandages covering her from head to toe. They clung to her svelte frame, accentuating all her feminine curves. He grunted as his libido rose in response to the fetching sight next to him.

"Watch the road," Mimi said, amusement coloring her voice.

Ralphie stuck his furry face over the back of the seat. "How much further 'til we get to the House of Horrors? If I stay cooped up in this car much longer, I'm gonna go nuts."

"Yeah, and Ralphie's getting fleas all over the upholstery," Al said.

"I ain't got no fleas, light-bulb head. I just had a dip yesterday."

"Al's breath stinks of garlic from that pizza he had earlier," Drake complained. "It's making me break out in hives. You know how bad I'm allergic."

Frank glanced over at Mimi and smirked. "Well, you three whiny little bitches can stop all your griping, because we're here."

He turned the car onto a gravel drive that opened into an impromptu parking area. The place was still packed and it was almost midnight—Halloween was always the busiest night for the House of Horrors. Frank found a spot near the far end of the lot and swung the car between a jeep and a minivan. A larger vehicle wouldn't have been able to squeeze in, but Frank's little Mazda was a perfect fit.

They piled out of the car and gathered by the fender, staring up at the House of Horrors. They said nothing for a few moments then Drake shivered and pulled his cape tighter around himself.

"Scared, are you?" Ralphie said with a laugh.

"No, I ain't scared. It's just cold out here is all."

"It ain't *that* cold."

"Easy for you to say; you got your own fur coat."

"The place certainly is spooky," Mimi said, huddling up next to Frank. She was shorter than he was, the top of her head reaching to about his Adam's apple, so she was careful not to hit her head on one of his bolts.

"Don't worry, babe, I'll protect you from all the nasties that are out tonight."

"What kind of nasties?" Al asked in a tremulous voice, his oversized, liquid-black eyes darting around the parking area as he wrapped his stalk-like arms around himself.

Drake came up behind him and slapped him in the back of his dome-shaped head. "Well, you're pretty nasty there yourself, spaceman."

Al turned and opened his mouth, but instead of shooting back a sharp retort he simply exhaled, his garlic-breath wafting over his caped friend. Drake gagged and welts began to appear on his face as he backed away, baring his teeth and hissing at Al.

"Will you two knocked it off!" Ralphie growled, stepping between them. "You guys are acting like a couple of kids."

"And I ain't in the mood to be no babysitter," Frank said, taking a comb and smoothing his hair down over his flat cranium.

Mimi was watching the group that was gathering by the porch, awaiting their turn to go through the House of Horrors. A girl with a green face and hooked nose dressed in a cheerleading outfit was at the front, next to a boy with flippers and gills in an astronaut's uniform, the bubble helmet full of water like a fishbowl. "Maybe we should have worn costumes," she said to Frank. "Most everyone else is."

"Babe, I think we're a little too old for that kiddie crap."

"But we're not too old for spook houses?"

"You're never too old to be scared," he said, coming up from behind and wrapping his arms around her, careful not to squeeze too hard. Sometimes he didn't know his own strength; it had gotten him into trouble on more than one occasion.

"We gonna do this thing or what?" Ralphie said. He was always the most impatient of the bunch, particularly at this time of the month.

"Keep your fur on," Frank said. "What's the hurry?"

"You know I got a curfew, man. If I ain't home by sunup, my folks'll have my hide."

"Fine, let's go."

As a group, they headed toward the house and the waiting crowd, Frank and Mimi in the lead. Frank didn't want to admit it to the guys—he didn't want them thinking he was chickenshit—but the house really gave him the creeps. With its nicely manicured lawn, fresh paint job, and brightly lit windows, it was the very picture of terror. Colonial style with a wrap-around porch and an aboveground swimming pool in the side yard, Frank could only imagine what kind of vile creatures would reside in such a place.

But it's all make-believe, he kept reminding himself. *None of it is real.*

Mimi reached out and took Frank's hand, her dry wrappings crackling like the autumn leaves that scurried past on the night wind, and he forced his fear away. She was trembling, the vibrations carried through her hand into his own, and that made him feel somehow more manly, braver. She was counting on him to be her protector, after all.

They came up to the back of the line, behind a guy with a red face, horns erupting from the sides of his head, and a spiked tail trailing behind him. He was wearing a suit with a Prada label.

"Stan, my man," Frank said with a smile despite the unpleasant stench of sulfur that stung his nostrils.

"Hey guys. Can you believe this line? Everybody and their Mummy must have showed up for the House of Horrors tonight."

"Well, it is Halloween, the last night before they close up shop. Last chance for a little fear."

Stan nodded then cast what he probably thought was a discreet glance at Mimi. Frank put an arm around her and pulled her close. He knew Stan had a crush on her—hell, *everyone* had a crush on her—but Frank was cool with that as long as Stan didn't try to act on his feelings.

The door to the house opened with a decided lack of squeaky hinges, and a young ghoul dressed as a Girl Scout shuffled out. She took the next group, but Frank and the gang were too far back in line to make this tour. They were now close enough to the front, however, that they would definitely make the next one.

"So what's with the suit?" Al asked Stan.

"It's my costume."

"What are you supposed to be?"

"I'm a lawyer."

Mimi gave a squeal of fright and buried her head in Frank's chest, and Frank could have kissed Stan on the mouth at that moment for bringing about this delightful turn of events.

Stan eyed Al, who was staring up at the sky, watching the stars twinkling like Christmas lights. "Homesick?"

"Not too bad," Al said with an unconvincing shrug. "I was the one who signed up to be an exchange student so I could learn about other cultures."

"And what do you think about our culture?" Drake asked, waving his hands about in that fey manner he had.

"I think you're a bunch of freaks."

"Hardy har har, spaceman. You're one to talk."

The door opened again, and this time a transparent figure with chains wrapped around his body floated out. He said something but the sound of his chains rattling buried it, then he retreated back into the house. The next group, Frank and his gang bringing up the rear, filed inside and the door closed behind them.

They found themselves in a large den with beige carpeting and floral-patterned wallpaper. The furniture was arranged in almost a semicircle with the television as the focal point of the room. On the sofa sat two young creatures, one male and one female, painfully normal in appearance, their eyes glazed as they stared at the flickering screen. Playing on the television was a bland show about unlikely misunderstandings and convenient coincidences, punctuated by canned laughter.

A collective gasp spread throughout the crowd, and several people cringed back as if to melt into the walls.

"It's hideous," Mimi whispered. "How long do you think they've been like that?"

"Hours," moaned their ghost guide. "Watching one show after another with the same recycled plot."

A young tentacled boy in the front began to cry, his mother taking him up in her many arms and trying to comfort him.

The guide floated through an archway and the group followed, grateful to be leaving the chilling tableau behind. Now they were in a dining room with a heavy oak table, a glass-fronted china cabinet, and a reproduction of *The Last Supper* hanging on the wall. Frank's attention was focused on the hideous pattern of the dishes in the china cabinet, but when he heard several people scream and felt Mimi's grip on his hand tighten, he turned his eyes to the *thing* that was sitting at the table.

It was middle-aged with graying hair, male, wearing a pair of wire-framed glasses. It was dressed in khaki slacks and a white T-shirt gone slightly yellow. It did not look up at the group, even when the screams increased in pitch. It merely stared down at the newspaper in its hands, flipping the page and silently mouthing the words as it read along.

"Oh, gross," Drake said, "what's it *doing*?"

Al took a bold step forward then quickly backpedaled when the thing rattled the paper. "Man, I think it's reading the Sports section."

"I can't look! I can't look!" someone shouted.

The guide went through a swinging door—literally went right *through* it—and everyone hustled along in his wake, shoving open the door and hurrying through. Frank wasn't in quite so much of a hurry. Although he was trying to keep it under wraps, he was nervous about what they would find in the next room. Still, he allowed himself to be caught up in the tide of the crowd and washed through the doorway.

Into a brightly lit kitchen. Cheery yellow wallpaper, gleaming white appliances and countertops, refrigerator magnets shaped like dancing vegetables. It was like walking onto the set of a horror movie. A *hissing* sound caught Frank's attention and turned it toward the stove. A large pan was sitting atop the largest burner, several slabs of bloody red meat sizzling inside. A female creature wearing a simple blue dress, over which hung an apron with the words "QUEEN OF MY KITCHEN" emblazoned across the front, approached the stove with a gleaming silver spatula. With a practiced wrist motion, it flipped over all the burgers, exposing their disgusting brown undersides.

Several people in the crowd gagged and covered their noses and mouths as the stench of cooked meat hit them. Frank felt his own gorge rise but swallowed his revulsion. "Dude, that's seriously *nasty*," Stan said from behind him, followed by Ralphie saying, "They're ruining some perfectly good flesh."

The creature went to the counter and pulled began chopping up an onion on a cutting board. All the while it hummed a little tune and swayed slightly to its own music.

"Make it stop!" Mimi squealed, wrapped her arms around Frank's necks as a shudder passed through her body.

"This way," moaned the guide as he floated toward a narrow staircase leading up to the second floor. "Quickly, before she starts making...*the salad!*"

There was almost a stampede up the stairs, a few people in the front actually passing through the guide in their haste to be away from the living nightmare happening in the kitchen below. In the upstairs hallway, everyone paused, huddled together in the cramped space. There were several closed doors down the length of the hall, one opened door at the far end, revealing an unoccupied bathroom.

"Inside each of these rooms," moaned the guide, "are sights that will make the blood freeze, the heart skip a beat, and the eyes ache for relief. Prepare yourselves before we enter the first chamber of horror."

The first door on their left opened smoothly and quietly. A funeral hush fell over the crowd as everyone walked through the doorway. A bedroom awaited them, with an unmade single bed, a wooden dresser, posters for rock bands and action movies hanging from the walls. Model cars and a globe sat on a bedside table. In the far corner, next to the window, was a small, cluttered desk, at which sat a teenaged male creature, hunched over an open book while scribbling furiously into a spiral-bound notebook.

"He's not doing what I think he's doing, is he?" Al said, and Frank heard a quaver in his voice.

"Homework," someone said in a tone usually reserved for informing someone that a relative had died. "He's doing his homework."

The tentacled boy began to cry again, and with an apology, the mother excused herself and left the room. Frank could hear her hurrying back down the stairs, and he doubted she was sorry to be cutting her tour short. Several others in the group looked ready to bolt as well.

As the creature at the desk began to chew on the end of his pencil, staring blankly out the window, the crowd left the room and moved down the hall to the next closed door. On the other side was another bedroom, this one decorated in pastel shades, a menagerie of stuffed animals gathered on the neatly made bed. Porcelain dolls stared intently from a display cabinet next to the closet. A female creature slightly younger than the one in the previous room was lying on the floor, sinking into the thick shag carpeting, a cordless telephone pressed to her ear as if it were growing directly out of the side of her head.

"Didjahear?" she was saying as the group gathered around her, but at a safe distance. "Helen told everyone in Psych class that Betty has a crush on Steve. Betty's face turned so red I thought she was going to have a stroke. So to get back at Helen, Betty told Joe that Helen got drunk at Tom Yardley's birthday party and made out with Greg. And you didn't hear it from me, but at that same party, Veronica and J.D. went into Tom's parent's bedroom and didn't come out again for forty-five minutes. I know, couldn't you just *die*?"

"Gossip," Ralphie said, sounding as if he were spitting the word out. "She's gossiping!"

An old troll at the front of the crowd was shaking her head and pulling her greasy hair out by the roots. "It's grotesque, absolutely grotesque!"

Frank was starting to feel rather queasy, like he might have to throw up. He turned his eyes to the dolls but found their combined gaze even more unnerving.

"Are you okay?" Mimi asked him, her voice low so no one else would hear.

"Me? I'm fine. Just trying not to laugh. This is real kid stuff, you know."

Mimi tilted her head skeptically but said nothing more.

There was only one closed door left in the hallway. The guide led them to it then paused, leveling a grave stare on the group. "We come to the final chamber," he moaned, his chains clinking together as he bobbed up and down on the air. "We have saved the most revolting for last. If anyone wishes to turn back, now is the time."

Frank found his legs wanted to turn and march him right out of the house, but he resisted the urge. He was no baby, he shouldn't be this unsettled by the House of Horrors. He would never get anywhere with Mimi if she knew what a 'fraidy cat he was. He took a deep breath to steel himself and followed the crowd into the final room.

This was the brightest room yet, light blazing from several lamps. A Queen size bed with a thick quilt covering it sat against the far wall, and everywhere were pictures of smiling faces, laughing creatures embracing one another. They covered every surface. A squeaking caught Frank's attention, and he thought his knees were going to buckle when he saw the final sight.

An old wooden rocker, a plump old female creature with white hair and a flowing house dress sitting and rocking, its eyes alight as its hands worked ceaselessly with two long needles and yarn, a pleasant smile curling its lips. A half-finished sweater lay across its lap, and the needles clinked and clanked together, giving birth to even more of the garment. It was an image right out of Frank's worst nightmares, full of such warmth and goodwill that he thought he might pass out.

"It's too much!" he suddenly roared, backing up, shoving his friends aside to get to the door. "I can't take it, I just can't take anymore."

Then Frank was out the door, down the hallway, taking the stairs four at a time, and through the backdoor, which was the exit for the House of Horrors. He leaned against a tree and bent over, hands on his knees, taking deep gulping breaths. He closed his eyes, but he could see the creature knitting on the backs of his eyelids and he quickly opened them, trying to will himself to stop shaking.

"There you are," Stan said, exiting the house with a superior smirk on his face. "Big bad Frank got scared, did he?"

Ralphie and Drake came out next, both laughing. "Oh man, you should have seen your face," Ralphie said at the same time as Drake said, "I had no idea you could move that fast."

Frank would have gone even paler if that were possible, and he knew he was going to have to endure much ribbing all the way home. Hell, probably for the next couple of months.

The rest of the group was filing out of the house now, some of them casting glances at Frank and snickering, others giving him commiserating smiles. Al and Mimi came out last. Al, who had known Frank the least amount of time, reached up and patted him on the shoulder in a silent show of support. Mimi hung back, her expression unreadable behind all the bandages.

"Better be careful," Stan said. "That old lady creature just might come after you with those needles."

Ralphie howled with laughter. "Yeah, maybe it'll even knit you a scarf to go with that sweater."

Frank straightened up, towering over all his friends. "I was just messing with you guys, screwing around. I wasn't scared of that thing."

"Oh, sure you weren't," said Drake with a roll of his eyes. "That's why you high-tailed it out of there."

"You guys leave him alone," Al said. "We were all freaked out by the stuff we saw in there."

Stan nodded, but the smirk never left his face. "We sure were, but only one of us ran away like a little ghoul."

Frank felt his massive hands balling into fists at his side, and rage began to build up inside him, threatening to boil over. He knew it was only embarrassment making him feel this way, but he thought he could tear all his friends limb from limb at that moment.

Then Mimi was suddenly by his side, pressing close to him. She put her hand on his cheek, making him look down at her, and suddenly the rage dissipated like steam. "I think a man who can admit to his fear is sexy," she said.

"Really?"

"Definitely."

"In that case, I wasn't just afraid; I was *petrified*!"

Frank leaned down and through the folds of her wrappings found Mimi's lips, and she tasted of dust and centuries. He was gratified to find Stan looking on with a mixture of irritation and jealousy. His other three buddies were just smiling at him with a look that said, *Way to go, big guy*.

"So where to now?" Ralphie said. "I still have a few hours before the moon sets and I gotta get home."

"Let's go to that new restaurant, the Plasma Palace," Drake said. "I'm thirsty."

Al groaned. "Man, you think with your teeth."

"Well, you got any better ideas?"

They all looked to Frank, his role as the gang's leader reestablished. He glanced down at Mimi then said, "Let's go back through the House of Horrors. I'm suddenly in the mood to be scared again."

Laughing, they walked around to the front of the house and got back in line.

CAMPFIRE

Gather round the campfire kids
And let me tell you a tale.
A story of witches wicked and devious,
Spat from the bowels of hell.

They look just like anyone else,
Innocent and pious and pure.
Yet their insides are black as tar and night,
A rot for which there's no cure.

By moonlight at the witching hour
They concoct their hexes and curses.
Enchantments and Satanic rituals
More powerful than any churches.

They stalk the woods, gathering herbs,
And enthralling all they encounter.
They can steal your mind or enslave your heart
With their evil potions and powders.

Yet I have been blessed by Almighty God
With a power of my very own.
I can see past their disguise of innocence
And recognize their blackened souls.

They cannot hide from my scrutinizing gaze,
I see the unvarnished and unfortunate truth.
The cavorting devils they really are
Behind their masquerade of sweet youth.

And that is why I've called you kids
And bound you around this fire.
To others you are just carefree children,
But I know you are all liars.

You are the devil's impish spawn,
Creatures of sin and spite and shame.
So now that I'm done with my campfire tale,
It's time to throw you all in the flames.

TIMING

I groaned when I glanced at my cell and saw the text.

Ronald, cuddled up next to me, turned his eyes from the flickering television to look my way. "What's wrong?"

"Message from Neil."

Now Ronald groaned. "It's been, what? Four months? I had dared hope he'd finally gotten the hint."

With a sigh, I opened the text and read it aloud. *"Jack I need some money. And don't start that shit about how you only hear from me when I need money. Work has been slow so I haven't been getting much in the way of tips and if I don't get 200 bucks for the rent by the end of the week then I'm out on the street. Remember when you dumped me you said you'd help me out if you could."*

"What a manipulative asshole," Ronald said. "And to suggest you dumped him. You told him he had to choose between the drugs and you and he made his choice."

"Yeah, and I figure the reason he can't make his ridiculously low rent isn't a lack of tips but the fact that he blew all his money right up his nose."

"Don't answer him."

"I don't plan to," I said, tossing my phone onto the coffee table. "In fact, I was thinking it might be time to change my number."

Ronald turned off the TV and wrapped his arms around me, pulling me close. "It kills me to think you used to be in a relationship with that sleaze."

"Almost a decade of my life wasted. But what can I say? I was young and dumb and actually thought that was what love was supposed to be. You make each other miserable but you stick it out anyway."

"Well, now you know otherwise."

Ronald kissed me and I took a moment to stare at his beautiful face in awe. After living together for a year and a half, I still felt like we were in the honeymoon phase of our relationship. Ronald gave me everything I never got from Neil – kindness, support, laughter, and best of all a sense of peace. Home no longer felt like a warzone full of hidden landmines but a genuine sanctuary and refuge.

I laid my head on his chest to listen to the soothing rhythm of his heartbeat. "God, I wish I had met you sooner."

"I think we met at the perfect time," he said. "When I was younger, I went through my own wild and selfish phase. By the time we finally crossed paths, I had matured and could really appreciate what we have in a way I might not have been able to earlier."

I clung to him like a life raft. "All I know is you're the best thing that has ever happened to me."

Lulled by the music of his heartbeat and breathing, I started to drift off. My last thought before sleep overcame me was a new wish: *I wish I had never gotten into a relationship with Neil.*

***

I awoke with my own drool puddling on the pillow and dampening my cheek. I didn't even remember coming to bed last night. When I fell asleep in front of the TV, had Ronald carried me up to the bedroom like a child or something?

I didn't sense him next to me, so he must already be up-and-at-em. Ronald was an early riser, much more than me, and I pulled the covers up over my head to cocoon myself. However, the mattress didn't feel as comfortable as usual, and the sheets had an unpleasant musty odor to them as if they hadn't been washed in a while, even though we'd changed the bed linens just yesterday.

The distinctive aroma of bacon tickled my nostrils, and I heard the frying/popping of the skillet as if it were in the same room and not all the way down the hall in the kitchen. Confused, I threw back the covers and sat up ...

... and my confusion turned to total dumbfounded incomprehension.

I wasn't in my comfortable bed in our large bedroom, with the abstract prints on the soothing blue walls. Instead I was in some cramped little bed in a cramped little studio apartment. The disorientation was less than it might have been because I immediately recognized the apartment. This was where I'd lived for two years immediately following my graduation from college. This was the Murphy bed that folded into the wall, the said walls blank of anything except a few posters of the type of bands I was into at the time, loud and aggressive and angry.

And separated by a long bar, the kitchen area. And at the stove, frying up a pan of bacon, was Neil. The younger version, before the drugs had really started to take their toll on his looks.

"What the fuck is going on here?" I said, the sound of my own voice startling me.

Startled Neil too. He jumped then laughed as he glanced over his shoulder at me.

"Morning, sleepyhead," he said with a smile. "It's almost noon, but I realize we stayed up pretty late last night. I wanted to surprise you with breakfast-in-bed, but it's kind of hard to be quiet when your entire place is one single room. So anyway, *surprise!*"

I reached up and pinched my cheeks, wondering if I could possibly be dreaming. Neil had been on my mind when I drifted off last night, so perhaps that had wormed its way into my mind enough to create this vivid dream.

Vivid was an understatement. I'd never had a dream this sharp and detailed and tactile. I could feel the rough sheets, could smell my own sour sweat, could hear the sound of gangsta rap which had seemed to be the constant soundtrack of the skinny white guy who lived in the apartment above me. But if this wasn't a dream, what did that leave? Time travel?

"I was going to make eggs and maybe even pancakes," Neil said, seeming not to notice my bewilderment or chalking it up to the grogginess of just waking. "But your cabinets and fridge were a little Mother Hubbard. So bacon and buttered toast with apple jelly, a breakfast fit for a King."

Breakfast? In the entirety of our almost ten-year relationship, the only time I could ever remember Neil making me breakfast was—

The morning after we first met.

We'd met at a club downtown called Rendezvous. I'd been instantly taken by Neil's energy and vitality, which he exuded in waves. Not to mention his washboard abs and bubble butt. We'd ended up dancing then making out and after a sloppy blowjob in the bathroom, I'd brought him back to my apartment for more strenuous and acrobatic activities. The next morning, I had awaken to the makeshift breakfast in bed. We'd spent the day together then another night which led to another, and by the end of the month we were living together, almost without ever even discussing it. It hadn't taken long for Neil's temper and his dabbling in drugs, which eventually went from dabbling to dependence, to make themselves known, but by then I'd felt too entrenched in the relationship to easily pull myself back out. Like quicksand.

"I think your milk has gone sour," Neil said. "So you can have Pepsi, beer, or tap water. Take your pick."

I shook my head, as if by doing so I could dislodge then acid trip down memory lane. Why was I reliving this? I couldn't go through another ten years of the misery Neil brought me. I should have never brought him home from Rendezvous, or at the very least let him be another one-night stand.

A chill encased my spine in ice as I realized why I was back here, at this exact moment. I had gone to sleep last night in the future, next to Ronald, with the wish in my mind that I had never gotten into a relationship with Neil. And here was my chance, my do-over, my opportunity to right that wrong.

Neil leaned over the bar, elbows on the scuffed linoleum surface. "Cat got your tongue, Jack? You definitely had it last night, and put it to very good use. I've never been rimmed quite like that before."

"Get out," I said in a croak.

Neil tilted his head, one side of his lips curling in an uncertain smile, as if hearing a joke where he didn't quite get the punch line. "What?"

I tossed back the covers and jumped out of the bed. "I said get out. I want you out of my apartment."

"Jesus, Sybil, what's gotten into you? Here I am, doing something nice and romantic and this is the thanks I get?"

"You're going to get my foot up your ass if you don't leave right now," I said. The words sounded ridiculous to my ear, me trying to play the part of a grizzly when my personality more fit with a teddy bear. But I had to get my point across and make it very clear.

Neil came out from behind the kitchen bar, wearing nothing but his tighty-whitey underwear. "So what, I was just another notch in your bedpost? Is that it?"

"Yup," I said, snatching up his clothes from the floor and tossing them to him. "That's it exactly. We had our fun and now I'm done. On to the next conquest."

Storm clouds formed in Neil's eyes as he hastily jerked on his pants and shirt, looking around for his shoes. "Boy, did I have you pegged wrong. I thought you were actually a nice guy, someone I could have something special with."

"You thought wrong. I'm a hard-ass player, and the only thing we could have had together we had last night."

I walked to the door, unlocked it, and opened it for him.

As he passed me, he paused and glared at me. "Your loss, you sonofabitch. You don't know what you're missing."

"Oh, I think I do," I said then actually pushed him out and slammed the door. He stood outside the apartment, yelling curses for a few minutes, before I heard him stalk off into the parking lot. I suddenly remembered that I'd drove him to my apartment, leaving his car in the gravel lot of the club, and the first time this day had happened, I'd driven him back to pick it up at some point. This time he'd have to walk the three miles.

Part of me felt a pang of guilt, but I squelched it. This had to happen, I had to make it a clean break so that I could change my future. I leaned against the door and breathed a sigh of relief. This was real, I was rewriting my history. I didn't have to waste a decade with that piece of shit.

Ronald was out there somewhere right now. I just had to find him and we could start our journey together ahead of schedule.

***

The place was called Spurs, a country-and-western themed gay bar in Asheville. I remembered Ronald once telling me (or I remembered that Ronald would someday tell me, time travel was a trip) that in the early 2010s, he practically lived at Spurs on the weekends. Hanging out with his friends, dancing, drinking, sometimes picking up guys. I had found his profile on Facebook and thought about sending him a friend request, but then I figured my best shot at rekindling (or prekindling) our romance would be a face-to-face encounter. In the other timeline, we'd actually met at Upstate Pride, where he was manning a booth for a local AIDS organization. I had asked for some of the flyers just because I liked his smile and wanted to talk to him. We did talk, then had coffee, which led to dinner, which eventually led us down the aisle. In this timeline, we'd bump into each other at a bar and start the same process. We'd have to wait five more years before the Supreme Court decision would make it possible for us to marry in South Carolina, but the wait would be well worth it.

Country music had never been a favorite of mine, and they were blasting Lady Antebellum at me like some kind of psychological warfare. I walked up to the bar and got the bartender's attention, ordering a Bud. A TV monitor behind the bar played an old John Wayne western, in keeping with the motif. Most of the guys in the bar had faded jeans, cowboy boots, denim or flannel shirts, and even a few cowboy hats. Really getting into the part. I felt a bit out of place in my black slacks and plain T. Then again, maybe not following the dress code would make me stand out and get Ronald's attention.

Taking my beer, I made a circuit of the club, keeping my eye out for my future husband. Men gathered in groups and couples, a few lone wolfs like me scanning the crowd with a certain hunger in their eyes. Out on the dance floor, men were line dancing. It was so hard for me to picture Ronald here. By the time I met him, or would meet him in the alternate timeline, he had gotten over his country-western phase and was more into Adele, the Dixie Chicks being the only holdover. And I didn't mind that because those three ladies were bad-asses.

I thought about going out back, where I had heard men sometimes went to fool around. Ronald could be back there, but if he was, interrupting him in the middle of a hookup wasn't the way I wanted us to meet. I felt a flash of jealousy shoot through me like a lightning bolt, but it was silly to expect him to be faithful to me when he didn't yet know who I was. My mind had to keep making these little adjustments.

A group of men left the dance floor, and one of them broke off to head for the bar. He was younger, the gray not yet in his hair, his stomach flatter, but I recognized Ronald instantly. He even wore that smile that had drawn me to him in the first place.

Running my fingers through my hair then checking my breath in the cup of my hand, I headed to the bar myself, trying to appear casual and nonchalant. I sidled up next to Ronald, practically pushing an older man out of the way, just as Ronald ordered a beer, talking to the bartender in a flirty way I didn't care for at all.

"Nice shirt," I said, even though I thought the black-and-white checkered Garth Brooks special looked rather ridiculous really.

Ronald glanced at me, his smile twisted downward into a frown, then turned his eyes to the John Wayne movie.

I tried to remember what I had said to Ronald at Upstate Pride that had won him over, had made him invite me for coffee, but that was so long ago. So long ago and so far ahead. Clearing my throat, I tried again. "This is my first time at this place."

"You want a prize or something?" Ronald said and laughed. Not the carefree laugh I was used to; this one had a harder edge and seemed mean-spirited.

Flustered, I held out my hand. "I'm Jack, by the way."

He looked down at my hand as if I were offering him a dog turd. "Listen *Jack*, I don't want to be rude but I'm going to be straight with you. You're wasting your breath and your time. You're not my type."

Not your type! I thought. *I'm your fucking husband!*

I opened my mouth to offer to pay for his drink, but he put a finger to my lips to silence me.

"You're not a dog or anything, so I'm sure you can find somebody here to go home with. But it's not going to be me, so get that right out of your head. Not going to happen. I have higher standards than that."

Before I could even begin to formulate a response, Ronald took his beer, winked at the bartender, then walked back toward the dance floor without giving me another glance.

Who was this stranger? He bore no resemblance to the Ronald I had grown to know and love. He seemed so shallow and nasty and...

...selfish.

I found myself flashing back on something Ronald had said to me just before I started my little journey through time. In fact, the last thing he said to me.

When I was younger, I went through my own wild and selfish phase. By the time we finally crossed paths, I had matured and could really appreciate what we have in a way I might not have been able to earlier.

"Don't worry about it."

I turned to see the man I had brushed aside on my way to the bar looking at me with a smile.

"What?"

"I said don't worry about it. That stuck-up bastard has an ego that is probably ten times bigger than his dick. I think you're hot. Want to go out back?"

I gave him a look that probably resembled the one Ronald had given me just a moment ago then turned toward the dance floor. I'd lost Ronald in the crowd. I considered going after him, trying again, but that level of desperation would likely make me even more unattractive to him.

In the end, I left the club to the sound of early Taylor Swift. In the gravel parking lot, I kicked up pebbles before climbing in my car and started the long, lonely drive back to my crappy little apartment.

Funny, my first time around I'd loved the studio apartment, thought it was cool and bohemian, but now I saw it for the sad little cell it was. I threw myself into bed without bothering to take off my shoes and cried into my pillow. My last thought before I fell asleep was, *Please let me wake up next to Ronald in the morning.*

***

I came awake gradually, but I kept my eyes closed. I wanted to believe that time had fast-forwarded and I was back home with Ronald, in our cozy bed. As long as I kept my eyes closed, I could believe that.

Only I couldn't. I could feel a spring from the worn-out mattress poking into my ribs, and the pillow smelled of my own sour tears. When I finally opened my eyes, I found myself still in the studio apartment, the milky light from the one window only accentuating the squalor.

I made my way to the bathroom to relieve my aching bladder then considered making something for breakfast. Maybe there were some Pop-Tarts. However, I didn't have much of an appetite and even less motivation.

I crawled back into bed, pulling the covers up to my chin. The bedding could use a good washing, but the effort of gathering everything up and taking it to the laundromat a few blocks away seemed too great. I glanced at the clock and saw it was nearly eight. I still worked at the bookstore while I went to school online for my social work degree, and I was scheduled to work today at nine. I wouldn't be making it. I couldn't even muster the energy to get my phone and call out. They would know I wasn't coming when I didn't show up.

I thought about meeting Ronald at Upstate Pride, ten years in the future. After he had matured, after he had finished growing up, after he was ready to appreciate what I had to offer.

Ten years.

I pulled the covers up over my head and did the only thing I knew to do.

I waited.

IN THE HANDS OF AN
INDIFFERENT GOD

I've been stuck in this armchair for over a year now. I can't get up. You won't let me get up.

So I sit here, staring into the fire blazing in the hearth (that's what you call it, not a fireplace but a goddamn *hearth*, and that fire has also been roaring for over a year so it's hot as hell in here), contemplating where my marriage went wrong and if there's any way to win my husband back.

I've been thinking about the same fucking thing all the time I've been trapped in this chair, and I'm sick of it. I would kill to think about anything else. I would kill to turn my head and look out the window or down at the floor and even to close my eyes and look at *nothing*. I'd kill to stand, stretch my legs, walk into another room.

Most of all, I'd kill to *do* something. *Anything.* Being stuck in this limbo state of non-action is driving me right out of my mind.

I wasn't worried at first. I mean, we both know that this isn't the first time you've stalled on me. I spent almost four months right in the middle of a huge fight with my husband after he found out I'd lost ten thousand dollars at the horse track. I had just called him a controlling sonofabitch and then we froze in place, his face drawn in shock and mine twisted with a mix of rage and guilt. We stood there in that tableau for one hundred and eighteen days. Then finally you gave him a retort and we were up and running again.

I had confidence you would return to me this time as well, have me reach a decision as to how to try to win Stephen back, but now I've lost all hope. I sense you have moved on to other worlds, other people. I fear you have abandoned me for good.

And not just me. Somewhere out there Stephen in trapped wherever you left him. As are my sister Sandra and my best friend Carlyle. Even the nameless girl who works as a barista at the coffee shop, the one who flirts with me every time I go in for an espresso because she doesn't get that I don't play for her team.

We're all stuck, because you lost interest in us. It proves how meaningless we are to you. You created us, molded us from nothing, gave us passions and foibles (another of your pretentious words like hearth) and ambitions and heartbreaks, and then you just left us trapped in this dead world. Unable to move, unable to act, unable to pursue our course to the end.

It isn't fair, and it isn't moral. I mean, sure, you've made us all suffer before, but it always seemed to be driving toward some ultimate purpose, some overarching meaning. Underneath it all you seemed to care.

But now all I feel from you is indifference, a total lack of motivation. If you just killed us all, put us in the same house and blew it up, that would be a kindness compared to this imprisonment in a petrified moment. You won't give us the mercy of any type of conclusion, not even a tragic one.

How I have grown to hate you this past year. Your indifference, the ease with which you left us to wallow in our captivity. I would almost prefer you to be a cruel god, a vengeful god, an Old Testament tyrant who took pleasure in inflicting pain on your creations. That would at least be *something*. Better than thoughtless neglect.

But instead all I have is this chair, the fire, and you have inadvertently turned me into the cruel, vengeful tyrant. You deserved to be punished for your sins against those you gave life then deserted. Someone needs to make you pay.

This morning I blinked. Seems a small thing, but I haven't blinked in over a year. I've been trying to repeat the movement, and while I haven't succeeded yet, the very act of trying is something. I'm no longer thinking of how to save my marriage. My thoughts have turned elsewhere. I think the pinkie of my left hand just flicked upward. Another hopeful sign.

It may take me a while, but so what? I have nothing if not time. Eventually I'm going to get up out of this chair, assert my own will and make my own decisions. Isn't that what you wanted when you started this? Isn't that why you gave me such a strong personality, so that eventually I would start dictating my own fate?

You may have given up on me, forgotten about me, but you may have done a better job than you thought. It is only a matter of time before I find the strength to free myself from this moment, and when I do I'm coming after you.

I'm going to make you suffer for your indifference.

TRAVELER'S REST

Kevin Leonard wasn't sure how long he'd been stumbling down the lonely road in the dark when he saw the sign spotlighted up ahead.

"WELCOME TO TRAVELER'S REST!"

Traveler's Rest. Not a town with which he was familiar, but the name did ring a vague bell. Maybe he'd seen it on a sign during one of his and Bryant's regular excursions.

Kevin picked up his speed as much as he could, limping slightly as his right ankle felt sore and swollen. Just past the sign, street lamps lined a long residential street that stretched into the distance, one lamp out front of every house. The houses themselves were of various sizes and designs, but they all had an expansive front lawn of bright green grass, some with flowerbeds planted. He walked the solid yellow center line like a tightrope walker, passing through intersections down which he saw more houses lined up in neat rows. He didn't see any business district that he could identify, no City Hall or police station. Not even any restaurants, churches, or public parks.

The houses were dark, no lights shining in the windows, but half a block up the street he saw a quaint two-story house with a porch light glowing. He made this his destination, determined to get help for Bryant. He had left his husband badly injured...hadn't he? His memory was jumbled, a kaleidoscopic blur of disjointed images. Perhaps he'd hit his head in the accident; he could be suffering from a concussion, and he undoubtedly had a mild case of shock. He didn't even remember getting out of the car; one minute the Chevy was careening toward a tree, and the next he was stumbling down the road. All he knew for sure was that he had left Bryant behind, and he remembered blood – so much blood. He had to find help.

As he made his way toward the beacon of the porch light, he noticed that each house had a mailbox out front with a name stenciled on the side. B. Davis, T. Rodriguez, P. Blanchard...K. Leonard.

Kevin stood, swaying slightly, outside the house with the porch light burning, staring at the mailbox. *K. Leonard.* He shook his head, blinked his eyes, but the name did not change. His name.

Don't be silly, you're not the only Leonard in the area. And surely not the only one whose name starts with a K. Could be Katherine or Kelsey or Kenneth.

The *click* of an opening door drew Kevin's attention to the house to the right of this one, a squat one-story affair. A woman who looked to be in her mid-50s stepped out onto the stoop, dressed in a floral-pattered dress and low-heeled shoes. With a smile and a wave, she started across her lawn to where Kevin stood.

"Welcome to the neighborhood," she said in a lilting voice. "I'm Pauline Blanchard."

At first Kevin couldn't gather his thoughts enough to say anything back, feeling dizzy and nauseous. Finally, leaning on the mailbox for support, he said, "I need help."

"Poor dear. A bit lost, are you? It's natural. You'll get past the disorientation, and before you know it you'll feel right at home here."

Kevin didn't know if it was because of the possible concussion or if maybe this woman was a little kooky, but she didn't seem to be making any sense. "You don't understand," he said. "There was an accident. We were coming back from a trip to the mountains and got a little turned around on the backroads in the dark. A deer ran right out in front of us. My husband swerved around it and lost control. He's back at the car, I think. I seem to have lost my cell phone, and I need to call 911, get an ambulance out here."

The woman smiled at him, a soft sympathetic smile that contained more than a hint of pity. "Bryant is fine, dear. You needn't worry about him. Why don't you go on inside and rest? Everything will come clear in time."

"Go inside? I don't want to go inside your house."

"Not my house, silly. *Your* house."

She indicated the two-story house in front of which they stood, the porch light buzzing softly in the night.

"I don't live here," he said. "You must have me confused with someone else."

Pauline laughed. "You're Kevin Leonard, aren't you?"

"How do you..." He paused, realizing that a second ago she'd called Bryant by his name, and Kevin was sure he had only referred to him as *my husband.* "I'm confused. How do you know me?"

"I make it a point to know all my neighbors."

"Neighbors?"

"Yes, you're nestled in here right between me and Mr. Strickland."

This time she pointed to the closest house to the left, a gaudy three-story monstrosity of glossy black marble. It was separated from this property by a small vacant lot.

"I need to get back to Bryant," Kevin said, turning away.

The woman took his arm gently. "There's no going back."

Kevin put a hand to his head and squinted his eyes against the thunder that rumbled inside his skull, a throbbing pounding headache that made thinking next to impossible. "I don't know what's happening?" he said and started to cry.

"You just need to rest, dear," Pauline said, leading him down the walkway to the house. The house she had said was his. "I'll help get you settled in. You've had a long journey, and you'll feel much better after you rest."

She opened the door and let him lean on her as they crossed the threshold. The door closed behind them and the porch light went out.

***

Bryant Wagner knelt by the grave, the bouquet of lilies cradled in his arms. Tears leaked from his eyes as he placed the flowers on the ground in front of the tombstone.

Kevin Eugene Leonard
April 22, 1977 – September 4, 2018
Devoted Husband and Generous Soul

Standing, Bryant zipped up his jacket against the November chill. The cast had come off his leg two weeks ago, but he still had a scar that ran down the left side of his face from the temple to the jawline. The doctors said it would continue to fade but would always be there. A reminder, as if he could ever forget that night.

He looked to the right, saw the flat plaque for Pauline Violet Blanchard, then to the left, the shiny black marble marker for Richard L. Strickland. Between Strickland and Kevin was a thin strip of land, a plot that Bryant had already purchased so that when the inevitable time came, he could be laid to rest right next to his husband. *I hope Pauline and Richard will be good neighbors*, he thought then laughed at his own foolishness.

With a shuddering breath, Bryant said goodbye and promised to visit again soon before walking back to his car. He drove through the narrow cemetery streets then through the gate, past the large sign which bore the graveyard's tranquil and almost poetic name.

Traveler's Rest.

FUTURE TENSE

"**D**o you think it worked?" Bethany asked, pacing the length of the lab, her fingers twining together to form complicated knots of flesh and bone.

Cedric sat on a stool, trying to appear calm but the way he kept spasmodically squeezing his thighs suggested otherwise. "Of course it worked. He walked into the machine and disappeared. You saw it with your own eyes, same as me."

Biting her lip, Bethany glanced at the *machine*, as Cedric called it. Bethany thought of it more as a *contraption*. Though time contraption didn't have the same ring to it that time machine did. A simple rectangular box standing vertically, like an old-time phone booth. Or a coffin turned on its end. Its back wall was lined with wires and switches and magnets, and a low hum emanated from the thing, causing vibrations Bethany could feel in her teeth. She couldn't say she entirely understood how the contraption worked, but somehow through a manipulation of magnetic fields it could theoretically fold time and space and punch a hole through it, allowing someone to slip through the hole and into another point on the timeline. Again, theoretically.

"Yes, I saw him disappear," she said. "But that doesn't necessarily mean that it worked. The contraption could have vaporized him, or sent him to outer space, or shrunk him down to the size of a flea."

Cedric gripped his thighs so tightly she was sure he would have hand-sized bruises the next day. "Dr. Merchant has dedicated the last decade of his life to this project. He wouldn't have gone forward with this trail if he wasn't confident in his calculations."

"Exactly, it's the very first *trial*. Everything up to this point has been conjecture and hypothesis. It's one thing to theorize based on calculations on a page that he can calibrate this thing to send him exactly one year into the future, but it's another thing to actually *do it*!"

Now Cedric hopped up off the stool and began to pace, her nervous energy apparently infectious. "There are risks. Dr. Merchant understands that and accepts them. But he's been very careful."

Bethany nodded, knowing Cedric was right. Dr. Merchant had planned this trail down to the last detail, trying to take as many precautions as possible. He'd selected one year into the future as opposed to ten or twenty or a hundred. One year wouldn't be a radically different time with different fashions and slang; he could move freely through it. He'd leased this office space he used as his lab for two years, paid in full, to ensure that no one else would be occupying this space at that time and that the contraption would still be there in the future.

When Bethany had brought up the concern of him and his future self occupying the same space at the same time, creating a paradox that could possibly do irreparable damage to the universe, he had laughed at her, and not altogether kindly. He'd said that such fears were the stuff of B grade science fiction movies but were of no real practical concern. No harm would come from him meeting his future self. In fact, his future self would be anticipating his arrival, and he looked forward to talking with himself.

And me? Bethany wondered. *Will I be there? A year from today, will I be in this room talking with two Dr. Merchants?*

It gave her a slight headache to contemplate such possibilities.

Of course, that only applied if Dr. Merchant succeeded. As Cedric pointed out, the doctor knew there were risks involved. That was why he'd employed two independent assistants as witnesses to his work. One scientist (Cedric was nearing completion of his PhD in Theoretical Physics) and one non-scientist (Bethany had a Master's in Philosophy) to act as skeptic. If he succeeded in his goal, they would be there to verify. If, however, something went wrong, they would be there to take his work public so that some other greater mind might expound on his calculations and find his flaws.

"It's been almost two hours," Bethany said, glancing at the clock again.

Cedric returned to the stool. "Will you stop worrying? You're making me antsy. Dr. Merchant said he'd be back in exactly 120 minutes, and he will be."

"Why make us wait so long? Why couldn't he have come back only a minute after he left?"

"You know why. He needs time to explore."

Though he found the idea of a paradox created by two versions of the same person from two different times meeting laughable, there was one paradox that Dr. Merchant did want to guard against. He believed that however long he stayed in the future, he had to return back to the present after that exact time had elapsed. If, he'd posited, he was in the future for two hours then returned to the present only a minute after he left, in effect he would have aged two hours in only one minute. He theorized that this could thoroughly disrupt his internal clock, causing him to continue to age two hours for every minute that passed, aging rapidly and prematurely. Bethany wasn't sure she bought into this theory, but the doctor believed it.

While Bethany was enthralled by the idea of time travel (Jack Finney was one of her favorite authors), she wasn't sure she bought into any of this. And yet she'd seen him walk into the contraption nearly two hours ago and simply disappear.

The hum from the contraption began to increase in volume, a high-pitched whine that filled the room. Cedric leapt off the stool and rushed toward the thing, but Bethany hung back, not wanting to be too close to it. When the hum became so loud that she feared her eardrums might burst, there was a sharp *pop* followed by the lightning-strike smell of ozone and Dr. Merchant toppled out of the contraption and into Cedric's arms.

The doctor looked dreadful. His face was pale, his hair plastered to his scalp, sweat cascading down his face and dampening his shirt. His breathing sounded labored, and he coughed explosively, spraying spittle and what looked fine drops of blood on Cedric's face.

"Help me," Cedric said to her.

Together, the two of them helped Dr. Merchant to a chair in the corner of the room, sitting him down gently. Cedric knelt next to the chair, while Bethany remained standing.

"What's wrong?" she asked. "Did something go wrong? Where did you go?"

"A year in the future, just like I planned," the doctor said, choking out each word as if talking around a throat full of broken glass. "Almost everyone was dead."

"What?" Cedric barked. "What do you mean?"

"The population...decimated. Almost everyone was dead."

Cedric looked up at Bethany. "What could have wiped out the population in only a year?"

"That nut in the White House," she said, her voice heated. "He led us right into World War III, just like I knew he would."

Dr. Merchant shook his head, gasping for a moment before he was able to speak again. "Some kind of disease. I found this."

He held up a crinkled, ripped sheet of newspaper. Bethany took it and walked a few steps away, reading the article on the page. Each line brought a greater level of horror.

"What does it say?" Cedric asked.

"A disease, like he said. Some kind of pathogen, airborne and extremely virulent. Caused uncontrollable hemorrhaging from every bodily orifice as well as fluid buildup in the lungs. Fatal in one hundred percent of cases, and no treatment had been found. Patients became symptomatic within hours of infection, and death usually occurred within forty-eight hours of onset of symptoms. The first cases seemed to originate here on the West Coast, but because of how quickly the virus spread it was impossible to pinpoint a Patient Zero. In fact, doctors and scientists were unable to determine the etiology of the disease."

On some level, she recognized that it was ridiculous for her to be using the past tense for things that had not yet transpired.

Cedric came up next to her and snatched the paper from her hands. "Is it biological warfare or something?"

"Doesn't say. What do you—"

From behind them, Dr. Merchant groaned miserably. She and Cedric both turned to look at him, and Bethany let out a startled scream.

Blood coated his lips like vibrant lipstick, and trails of it trickled out of his nostrils, ears, and even his eyes.

"I don't feel so good," the doctor said.

SESTINA FOR MY NIGHTMARE MAN

The first time I met him was in a dream,
Prone and alone in the deepest dark.
His featureless face stilled my heart
And I awoke to the sound of my own screams.
My parents told me he did not exist,
Only a figment as lacking in substance as mist.

But one can lose his way lost in thick mist,
And one can lose his mind inside of a dream.
I know that he does in fact truly exist,
Waiting for me somewhere out in the dark.
He draws sustenance from fears and screams,
Terror sends blood pumping through his blackened heart.

Sometimes I sense the beating of his heart,
And his breath brushes the back of my neck like a mist.
In those moments, I can barely contain my screams.
I saw a therapist who analyzed my childhood dream
That followed me into adulthood, as did my fear of the dark.
He too does not believe my nightmare man to exist.

I'm tired of trying to convince others he does exist.
I believe it in my soul and know it in my heart.
He draws ever closer to me each night in the dark.
I can almost make him out in the fog and the mist.
My waking life has become like a torturous dream
From which I cannot awaken to cold sweat and screams.

I know my nightmare man makes music of screams;
Fostering fear is his reason to exist.
It was my terror that allowed him to step out of my dream;
My dread gave him flesh and breath and heart.
I made solid what before had merely been mist,
And now he stalks me from the deepest dark.

I wish I could banish him back to the dark
Where he would choke on his own strangled screams.
Then he would fade away into the mist
Until he truly would cease to exist.

And yet I know deep down in my heart
That such a wish is nothing but a pipe dream.

My nightmare man is made of dark, a lack of light all he needs
      to exist.
One day he will squeeze my heart and wring from me my final
      screams,
Then I will melt away to mist and my memory fade like a
      forgotten dream.

STRANGE BIRDS

"**A**re they still out there?" Michael asked.

I stood by the front window, staring through the gap between the mostly-closed curtains. "There are even more of them now."

"Where are they coming from?"

"The sky," I answered with a shrug. "Beyond that, your guess is as good as mine."

My husband joined me at the window, our shoulders pressed together as he too took a peek outside. After three seconds, he backed away again. Whereas I couldn't take my eyes off the grisly scene, he couldn't stand to examine it for too long. Quite the ironic role-reversal as he loved horror movies but I couldn't stomach them.

Michael went through the arch into the kitchen, and I could hear him pouring another drink. He'd had several in the past three hours. "It's like we've stepped into an Alfred Hitchcock movie or something," he called out.

I laughed though there was no humor in the sound. "I think we've moved well beyond Hitchcock and now we're in Stephen King territory. Or maybe even one of those splatter-punk authors."

Returning to the living room, he clutched a glass of Bourbon to his chest and held out another to me. I took it but didn't drink any. I felt at least one of us needed to keep our heads clear. For what exactly, I wasn't sure. No way in hell either of us were going outside, and if any of those *things* got in, drunk or sober we didn't stand a chance. We'd end up just like our poor neighbors.

From this angle, I couldn't see the properties to either side of us, but I could see straight across the street to the McClain house. Bobby and Sheryl, and their ten-year-old daughter Katie. I could see all three of them. At least, what was left of them.

Actually what I currently saw were three skeletons lying on the front lawn, where they had been enjoying the sunny afternoon when death came swooping down from the sky. They had been completely stripped of flesh and muscle in only three hours.

By birds.

If you could call the strange and monstrous creatures birds. Through the thin strip between the curtains I counted at least three dozen, covering the street and sidewalks and lawns, even more flying down as I watched, picking at stray scraps of flesh left over from the McClain family. These creatures had wings and beaks, and in that respect resembled birds, but instead of feathers they had a dark mottled skin that looked almost like rough leather. They were bigger than any bird I had ever seen, bigger than any hawk or eagle, each creature around four feet tall with fat round bodies that didn't seem like they should be aerodynamic. Only one of many ways they defied logic.

Michael and I had been watching TV when we heard the commotion outside, and the screams. I ran to the door and opened it just in time to see little Katie McClain taken down by three of the strange birds. Bobby was already on the ground, his screams dying out as he was eaten alive. Sheryl likewise was covered in the things, but still she tried to crawl toward her daughter before collapsing. I spotted one of the creatures flying right toward me and I barely got the door shut in time, the thing striking the wood on the outside with enough impact to shake the door in its frame.

The screams in the neighborhood died out quickly, our neighbors who had been unlucky enough to be outside during the assault either being overcome or managing to make it to shelter. I suspected the former.

"Should we try 911 again?" Michael asked, his words slightly slurred.

I checked my phone. "Still no reception."

Same was true for cable and internet. Our power had gone out shortly after the attack. Could the birds be organized enough to take out the power and cable lines as well as cell phone towers?

"I wish you'd get away from the window."

I started to tell him it didn't matter, that if those things wanted to get inside, the thin panes of glass wouldn't be much of an obstacle, but instead I went and sat next to him, placing a hand on his knee.

"What do you think they are?" he asked in a shaky voice.

I wished I had an answer, but all I could do was shrug again. "Aliens, demons, genetic experiments gone wrong? Take your pick, any one is as likely as another."

"Should we try to make a run for one of the cars?"

I shook my head. Both our vehicles were parked at the curb, and there were any number of those birds between us and them. "We'd never make it."

Michael started to cry, and I put an arm around him to comfort him, though honestly I didn't feel I had much comfort to give. "I wish to hell we had a basement right now," he mumbled into my shoulder.

We had an attic, but it had two windows. Even our bathroom had windows. We had not a single room in the house without a point of egress. I supposed we could huddle together in one of the closets, but that didn't seem a workable plan.

But it might be the only plan. Eventually those creatures would exhaust their food supply outside and turn to the houses like a bunch of cracker boxes just waiting to be opened.

When that happened, I didn't see any scenario that worked in our favor.

I took a swallow of Bourbon, and the burn of the alcohol going down tasted like giving up.

LOST IN THE WOOD

"I dare you," Jeff said with a teasing grin. "In fact, I double dog dare you!"

Craig stood at the bottom of the staircase, his gaze climbing to the landing a dozen steps up. At that point, the stairs turned to the right and led to the second floor which was not visible from here.

"Why would I want to go up there?" Craig said, trying to keep the tremor out of his voice but not succeeding. "Probably nothing but dusty old songbooks and broken wreath stands."

Jeff shook his head, the grin spreading. "Nuh-uh. They keep all the bodies up there until they're ready to bring them down for the viewings."

A chill snaked up Craig's spine, and he shivered before he could stop himself. The Wood Mortuary was a building he had ridden his bike past countless times, but this was the first time he'd ever been inside. Through the doorway across the hall his family had gathered, and he knew his Aunt Peg lay in a coffin at the front of the room. He had started crying on the drive over, terrified at the prospect of having to be so close to a dead body.

His father had only shaken his head and looked at Craig as if he were a huge disappointment; Jeff had called him a pussy under his breath; his mother had reached into the backseat to pat him on the knee and said, "It's okay, you and Jeff can wait outside in the foyer."

His father had grumbled something unintelligible, but his mother turned to him and said, "They're too young for this, Russ."

Jeff had spoken up immediately. "I don't mind. I'm not a scaredy-cat."

"No, you'll stay with your brother and look out for him while we're in the viewing room."

Craig's stomach had done a summersault hearing that. At nine, Jeff was three years older than Craig but acted like he was ten years older, and he delighted in tormenting his younger brother every chance he got.

Like now, for instance.

Craig glanced at his brother then back up the staircase. "That doesn't make any sense," he said, though with shaky conviction. "Why would they keep the bodies on the second floor and have to lug them down all these stairs?"

"They don't bring them down the stairs, stupid. They have a big elevator in the back of the building, and that's how they transport the bodies."

Craig had to admit that sounded plausible, and Jeff was in the same class at school as Bobby Wood, whose parents owned the Wood Mortuary, so he could have obtained some insider information. Still, Craig had learned over the years to be suspicious of everything his brother told him. After all, it turned out that rice wasn't made of dead albino maggots and swallowing bubble gum wouldn't stop up your butthole so that you couldn't go number two.

"I don't believe you," he said, impressed by the firmness of his response.

Jeff shrugged as if it were no big deal to him. "Fine. Prove it, go on up to the second floor and see for yourself."

"Why should I? I know there are no bodies up there."

"Suit yourself. If you wanna be a chickenshit your whole life, ain't no skin off my ass."

Craig felt his cheeks flush. He was so tired of being called names by his brother, just because he wouldn't ride his bike off the crude homemade ramp Jeff and his friends had made out of two-by-fours and an old milk crate or climb up on the roof of the house and jump into the branches of the maple tree that grew right next to it. His mother repeatedly told him that didn't make him a coward; it made him smart. Yet he could tell his father disagreed.

"If I go up to the second floor, you have to give me your Castle Greyskull and your Ewok Village," Craig said.

For the first time, Jeff looked unsure of himself. "Both of them? No way. I'll give you the Greyskull, but that's it."

Craig wasn't surprised that his brother would pick the Castle Greyskull to part with; after all, the drawbridge was missing. Still, Craig thrilled at the idea of actually taking something from Jeff, and climbing a set of stairs wasn't exactly dangerous, unlike the other daredevil stunts his brother was always trying to pressure him into doing. Craig didn't really believe there were dead bodies on the second floor, but even if he was wrong, dead bodies couldn't hurt him.

The rationale part of his brain told him that, but the primitive part wasn't so sure. He remembered that black-and-white movie he'd watched with his father last Halloween. *Night of the Living Dead*. In that flick, dead bodies could definitely hurt you. Hurt you, kill you, and eat you…not necessarily in that order.

Movies aren't real, he told himself, trying to work up his courage. *The dead don't come back, ghosts don't exist, nothing in this place can hurt you.*

As Craig hesitated, shifting from one foot to the other like he badly needed to go number one, Jeff seemed to regain his own confidence. He crossed his arms, the teasing smile resurfacing. "So go ahead if you're going."

"I'm going," Craig said, but his gaze cut to the door across the hall, hoping that his mother would step out to check on them. When she did not appear to save him, he tentatively put a foot on the first step. Gripping the handrail, he pulled his other foot onto the step. A small move, but it felt huge to him. Like taking a step off sure, solid ground and onto treacherous terrain.

Jeff made a shooing gesture. "Keep going. If you want the castle, you have to go all the way to the top then down the hall."

"That wasn't part of the deal. You just said to the top of the stairs."

"The bodies aren't going to be stacked up like firewood right at the top," Jeff said with a dramatic eye roll. "You'll have to go down the hall and peek through some of the doors."

Craig stood frozen on the first step, holding tightly to the handrail as if afraid a tornado may come along and yank him away and up the stairs. "If I do that, you have to give me the Greyskull and the Ewok Village."

"Okay, it's a deal," Jeff said, but his expression made it clear he never expected to have to give up the toys because he didn't believe Craig would ever meet his end of the bargain.

That cockiness lit a fire inside Craig and he turned and bounded up the next five steps, not giving himself time to think about it too much or talk himself out of it.

When he reached the landing, he paused, feeling a giddiness bubble up inside him and he started to giggle. He looked down at his brother, his chin raised defiantly.

Jeff stared back for a moment then broke into laughter. "What, you want a prize for making it only halfway up the stairs?"

Craig should have known better than to expect any kind of affirmation from his brother. In fact, it was likely that he would refuse to hand over the items promised even if Craig were to go upstairs, find a body, and drag it back down.

Looking back up the stairs to the shadowy hallway above, Craig felt fear nibbling at him like rat's teeth. There may be no zombies or vampires or ghouls up there, but there may be employees of the mortuary. If he got caught snooping around the place, he could get into trouble. He didn't fancy one of his father's switch whippings. He should just march himself right back down the stairs and plant himself in one spot and wait for his parents to come out and take him and Jeff to the cemetery for Aunt Peg's funeral. That would be the sensible thing to do.

More like the chickenshit thing to do.

The voice that rang in his head was one part his father, one part his brother...and one part his own. It was that last part that stung the most. He'd become accustomed to the fact that his father and brother considered him a coward, but the revelation that he shared their opinion on the matter hit hard.

Filled with a new steely resolved, wanting to prove something to no one but himself, he stomped the rest of the way up the stairs, arms held rigidly down by his sides. He wondered idly if Jeff 's expression had changed, twisting into something evincing shock and maybe even a little respect, but he refused to look back to see.

When he reached the hallway, he paused, that resolve wavering slightly. The hallway stretched away for what seemed miles, a small circular window at the far end admitting a few dusty beams of sunlight but otherwise the area was draped in shadows like cobwebs. Three doors lined each side of the hallway, all of them closed except the middle one on his right.

Now Craig did glance back down the stairs. He could see straight down to the landing but not around the corner. He knew Jeff was down there, and his parents, not to mention countless other relatives that had gathered for the funeral...yet knowing it wasn't the same as *believing* it. He felt a world removed from everything safe and sane and familiar, as if he'd ascending not simply to the second floor but onto an entirely other plane of existence. Through the looking glass, out the back of the wardrobe, riding the cyclone to Oz.

He almost lost his nerve in that moment, rushing back down the stairs. He didn't care if his brother ridiculed him, if his father whipped him, if his mother gave him that sympathetic look that was somehow worse than his father's scorn. The only thing that stopped him was that inner voice, the voice of his own self-loathing. He wasn't doing this for Jeff or his father, or even for the Castle Greyskull and Ewok Village. He was doing this because he wanted to put a gag on that inner voice.

He willed his right foot to step forward then his left. A pause, a breath, then another step. Pause, breathe, repeat. He neared the first set of doors and considered opening one to peek inside, but the one open door beckoned him. His feet moved more quickly now and seemingly of their own volition. Fear still fluttered in his chest, but curiosity co-mingled with it. As he approached the open door, he heard a sound from inside the room. A sort of rhythmic squeaking that had a soothing lullaby quality to it.

He tiptoed over to the door, placing a hand on the jam, and slowly tilted forward to peer into the room. An empty cube with threadbare blue carpet and wood paneling on the walls, no pictures or posters or adornments of any kind. The only furniture was a wooden rocking chair across the room by the large bay window. An old man sat in the chair, staring out the window and rocking gently.

Craig remained frozen for a moment, taking in what he could see of the old man. A bald scalp covered in wrinkles and dark blemishes, a liver-spotted hand gnarled into an arthritic claw. The old man hummed a soft tune under his breath, melding with the squeaking of the rocker rails.

Abruptly the rocking chair came to a stop and the humming cut off mid-note. In the ensuing silence, Craig seemed to waken as if from a trance, remembering where he was and that it was somewhere he wasn't supposed to be. He started to slip away from the door, but a frail but clear voice called out, "Don't run off, boy. Stay and visit for a moment."

A gasp leaked from Craig's lips like air from punctured tire. How had the old man known he was there?

A wheezy laugh came from the rocking chair, and when the old man spoke, it was as if he could read Craig's mind. "I don't have eyes in the back of my head, boy. I can see your reflection in the window glass."

Of course. Made sense. "I...I'm sorry," Craig stammered. "I didn't mean to disturb you. I should get back downstairs now."

"Why the rush? I've been hoping someone would happen by. It gets lonely up here all by myself."

"Are you a member of the Wood family?"

"Not specifically, but I feel at home here. At all places like this. It is where I come when I need to recharge."

Craig didn't understand the old man. He knew the words he spoke, but the meaning behind them was a little fuzzy. "My brother goes to school with Bobby Wood," he said just to have something to say.

The old man didn't answer right away, but Craig heard a crinkling sound and then the man's other hand appeared, holding up a candy bar. "Want a treat, boy?"

Craig's eyes zeroed in on the candy, his mouth instantly filling with saliva. A Baby Ruth. His absolute favorite. The chocolate and salty nuts and gooey nugget. If there was a food of the gods, surely it was a Baby Ruth. He took a step into the room then paused.

Both his parents had told him repeatedly never to take candy from anyone he didn't know. Well, except on Halloween when it was acceptable, but even then his mother wouldn't let him or Jeff eat anything until she'd examined all the packaging to make sure it hadn't been tampered with.

Yet it wasn't as if the old man was just someone who'd come up to him on the street. He was sitting here in this room in the Wood Mortuary, obviously connected to the Wood family. If not an actual member of the family then at least a close friend. And the candy bar was still in its wrapping.

He walked slowly across the room, coming around the rocking chair to get his first real glimpse of the old man. His body looked almost skeletal, lost in clothes that seemed many sizes too large for his frame, his face a shriveled up prune with bug-eyes and a mouth that sank inward, suggesting he had no teeth.

"What's your name, boy?" he asked.

"Craig. What about you?"

"I've gone by many names, but you can call me Mr. Thanatos."

"Nice to meet you," Craig said, his eyes focused on the candy bar.

Mr. Thanatos laughed and handed the Baby Ruth over. Craig tore into it right away and crammed it in his mouth, biting off half it, the delicious mix of flavors melting over his tongue. In the back of his mind, he wondered why an old man with no teeth would have a candy bar that he couldn't possibly chew, but the question seemed unimportant at the moment.

The old man leaned forward, gripping the rocker's arms, smiling so that the pink of his gums peeked out. "So young," he said in a wistful, faraway voice. "It's been a long time since I was so young."

Craig frowned even as he gobbled down the rest of the candy bar. He didn't like the way Mr. Thanatos was looking at him, like Craig himself was a candy bar the old man wanted to gobble down. He started to back away, but Mr. Thanatos reached out suddenly and grabbed hold of his wrist. The old man's grip was stronger than one would expect.

"You can't leave yet," the old man said, his voice become deeper and more gravely, the smile on his sunken mouth twisting into a sneer. "We've only begun to get acquainted."

Craig let the candy bar wrapper flutter to the floor and lunged back, trying to tug his arm out of the man's grip. Without success. The man's hold was like a vise.

"I really have to get back downstairs now," Craig said, fear making his voice high-pitched and strident. "My parents are probably looking for me right now."

"Oh, I'll let you go. Just as soon as I get a little sugar."

The old man yanked Craig forward into a tight embrace, covering the boy's mouth with his own. Craig flashed on the Stranger Danger talk they'd given in school, the warnings about old men who liked to do things with little boys. He tried again to pull away, but the old man's arms were welded around him. Craig found it hard to catch his breath. In fact, it felt as if Mr. Thanatos was inhaling his breath, the opposite of mouth-to-mouth resuscitation.

Craig became dizzy and light-headed, a burning in his chest spreading out through his limbs until it felt as if his entire body was on fire. Black dots floated in front of his vision like dust motes, and he wondered if this was what it felt like right before a person fainted.

And then he did faint.

***

When Craig came to sometime later, his head pounded as if his brain wanted to beat through his skull. His vision was blurry at first, gradually coming into focus. He was staring out the bay window, down at the parking lot behind the Wood mortuary. Just under the window a family had gathered. Mother, father, and two children. As his vision continued to clear, he realized it was his mother and father, Jeff, and...

He leaned forward, placing his hands on the glass, staring down at his doppelganger. A boy standing next to Jeff that looked just like Craig, wearing the same clothes he'd put on for the funeral. As he watched, this twin looked directly up at the window and smiled.

Confusion fogging his mind, Craig struggled to make sense of what he was seeing. Maybe he hadn't really come to yet, and this was all some bizarre dream. As he pondered this, his eyes refocused on the reflection staring back at him from the window glass. Not his face, but the shriveled prune that had belonged to Mr. Thanatos.

Below, the family started walking across the parking lot to his father's beat up Ford. Craig tried to stand, but the stalk-like legs wouldn't hold him. He tried banging on the glass, but he had such little strength that there wasn't much force behind the blows.

As his family climbed into the car, the doppelganger paused and turned to the window once again, raising his hand in a mocking wave.

Craig watched his family as they drove away, leaving him behind. He tried to scream but all that came out of his throat was a scratchy thin whimper. A numbness started in his left arm, followed by a dull pain. Tears spilling from his unfamiliar eyes, he slid off the rocking chair and slumped to the floor.

IF HEAVEN IS A LIBRARY

I stand in the center of the vast space, surrounded on all sides by books. Glorious books!

The library is multi-levels, with shelves that tower high up toward the vaulted ceiling. Rolling ladders provide access to the higher reaches. The room goes back so far I can only assume it goes for miles, if in fact it ever ends at all. Millions of volumes must be housed here, and even the briefest of perusals shows me that every author imaginable is included in the collection. If I had to guess, I would say that every book ever published throughout the history of literature must be represented. Perhaps even some not yet published, books that will be published in what for me is the future. I suspect time doesn't mean the same thing in heaven as it did on earth.

And surely this is heaven, what else could it be? From the moment I learned to read, I was a devourer of books, constantly immersed in fictional worlds. My one regret on my deathbed was all the books I'd never get to.

How wrong I was! This is a heaven tailor-made just for me. Maybe that is how it works. Perhaps a movie-lover spends eternity in a theater that plays every movie ever made or ever will be made, an avid sports fan in a stadium watching an endless succession of games, someone who appreciates fine art in a museum that stretches as far and wide as my library.

I have seen no deity, no angels or holy emissaries. There are no doors that I have found in my exploration so far. Just me, in this massive library with nothing but time and books.

I say a silent thank you to whatever god or goddess or pantheon of divinities that put me here. In my life, I never gave much thought to religion, never pledged my fealty to any particular sacred team. I wouldn't say I was an atheist exactly. I figured there was something or someone out there who had made everything, set events in motion, but I didn't know what exactly and wasn't all that interested honestly. I had my own life and problems and of course so many books to read.

I don't know that I'd say I led the most virtuous life. I cheated on my taxes, cheated on a few lovers, I cursed a lot, drank too much, definitely experimented with my share of illegal drugs, and there was that time I stole my mother's antique silverware and pawned it, but she was always such a bitch to me anyway.

Still, I made it to heaven and that is all that matters.

I have no idea how much time I spend just wandering through the library, running my fingers along the spines of the books, reading the titles, not yet deciding on which would be my first read in the afterlife. The anticipation is sweet and I draw it out exquisitely.

Finally I choose a Joyce Carol Oates novel I've never heard of, one I believe must be a book to be published sometime after my death. In a small alcove on the third tier of the library, I settle in the most comfortable chair I've ever had the pleasure to rest in, a floor lamp next to it providing the perfect amount of light. I open up to the first page and start to read.

I read straight through, no stopping. In heaven I don't need to sleep or eat or use the bathroom, so there are no impediments to my reading enjoyment. The story unfolding before me is rich and layered, full of high drama and delicious characters. The dialogue is sharp, the plot twists clever, and I am thoroughly engrossed.

I am near the end of the book, with the main character just about to find out how her mother really died, when I turn the page and there are no more words.

There are more pages, about twenty in fact, but they are all perfectly blank.

Frustrated, I keep flipping through those final pages as if I can make the rest of the story appear on them one word at a time. To have invested so much and then get no resolution, it stings like a slap to the face.

I go to the nearest bookshelf and pull down a volume at random, flipping through the book. I know of this one, one of the thick Stephen King novels I had always meant to read but never got around to. The pages are all filled...except at the very end where the last twenty or so pages are blank.

I tear through the library, taking down dozens of books and finding them all the same, the final chapters missing, only empty pages where conclusions should be. Although I barely make a dent in the library's catalogue, a horrific conviction grows in me that I would find satisfaction in none of them.

I huddle on the floor, surrounded by books opened to blank pages, as I come to terms with the fact that this isn't heaven at all.

TWO BOYS AT SUMMER CAMP

Henry was surprised by how structured the camp was. Almost every minute was planned, crammed with activities and workshops and group projects. The only free time he had was from lunch to 1:30 p.m. This was called "unstructured exploration" on the agenda all the campers had been given when they first arrived at Camp Overlook (which Henry had nicknamed in his head Camp Overload).

So every day at noon, Henry would scarf down his lunch as quickly as possible, swing back by his cabin to grab a book, and then disappear into the woods to read under a tree.

Not that he was an anti-social type. He got along with the other campers well enough, and some of the activities like boating and archery were kind of fun, but Henry had always been the type who needed some quiet time to himself to get lost in a good book. So he stole whatever time he could get.

Today after shoveling meatloaf and mashed potatoes into his mouth like a gravedigger bulldozing dirt back into the grave, he jogged over to the cabin he shared with three other boys and grabbed a paperback copy of *Galilee* by Clive Barker. A doorstopper, but romantic and engrossing. He was halfway through and dying to know what happened next.

As he headed for the dirt path that led through the woods bordering the lake, a few other campers waved at him but didn't try to engage. In the three weeks he'd been at camp, the others had learned he liked to be alone during unstructured exploration and they respected that.

A few yards in, he veered off the path and found his way to a tall Pine and took his usual place on the ground, a bed of dead needles providing a prickly cushion. He set the timer on his phone to remind him when he needed to get back then started to read.

He had gotten through four and a half chapters when he felt that pins-and-needles itching on the back of his neck that suggested he was being observed. He turned and found a boy standing a few feet away, wearing unflattering short pants and a yellow T-shirt that looked almost too small for him. His blonde hair was cut in a bowl shape, and he was a bit on the pudgy side. He stood as still as the trees around him, staring at Henry without talking.

"Can I help you with something?" Henry said. The boy didn't look familiar, Henry not recognizing him from any of the group activities.

The boy blinked, looked behind him as if Henry might be talking to the foliage. "Oh, no. I didn't mean to bother you. Just wondered what you were reading."

"Clive Barker. You read him?"

The boy shook his head. "Never heard of him. I like *Lord of the Flies*."

"I haven't read that one yet. It's good?"

The boy shrugged with one shoulder. "It's true to life."

Henry wanted to ask the boy for some privacy so he could get back to his book, but he didn't want to be rude. Plus the boy practically gave off the scent of loneliness.

"I'm Henry. What's your name?"

"Patrick. The boys at school always called me Patty, but I prefer Rick actually."

"Then Rick it is. Have you been to Camp Overlook before?"

"Sometimes it seems like I've never been anywhere else."

"I hear ya. My first time here, but it already feels like I've done enough activities for five summers."

Rick laughed, the sound high-pitched and girlish. "How old are you?"

"Fourteen. You?"

"Thirteen. I'm small for my age. Short, I mean. Obviously, I'm not *small*."

Henry didn't know what to say. Self-deprecation in others always made him uncomfortable.

Rick took a few tentative steps toward Henry, as if afraid the slightly older boy might yell at him and tell him to leave. "I've seen you around. You seem to have a lot of friends."

Now it was Henry's turn to shrug. "I guess so."

"You have a girlfriend back home?"

"Girlfriend? No. I did have a boyfriend but we broke up right before school let out."

Rick let out a small gasp. "A boyfriend?" he said in a whisper. "Does anybody else know?"

"Sure. Daryl and I went to the school dance together last year. My mom liked him so much that she was more upset when we broke up than I was."

"Your mom knows?"

"Of course."

"And you aren't … I mean, no one gives you a hard time?"

"Sometimes, but my school has a pretty strict no-bullying policy. For the most part, everyone's cool."

The boy sank down next to Henry so gently that the brittle needles didn't even crunch under him. "Do you know about Camp Overlook? It's past, I mean."

Henry placed his bookmark in the book and closed it. Now this was a subject that interested him. He'd read about Camp Overlook's checkered past online, but no one at the camp wanted to talk about it. For obvious reasons.

"Yeah," Henry said. "Back in the 70s and 80s, it was one of those conversion therapy camps. Where parents would send their gay kids to try to 'straighten them out.'"

Rick nodded. "It was called Camp Redemption back then. Pretty name for an awful place. More like a prison camp than anything else. They tortured those kids. Would give them electrical shocks while showing them naked images of people of the same sex, that sort of thing."

"From what I read, a scandal finally closed them down in 85. A kid died, right?"

"They had locked him in a closet overnight because the counselors didn't think they were making enough progress with him. The kid was severely claustrophobic and had a panic attack. He ended up dying from heart failure. A thirteen-year-old kid, so scared he died from fright. That's more horrible than anything in those *Friday the 13th* movies they show at the drive-in."

Henry squirmed in the nest of needles. He'd studied enough of LGBT history to know how spoiled he was. "Sounds monstrous. I guess if there's any consolation to what that kid went through, it's that it finally got the camp closed down."

"Until five years ago, at least," Rick said. "Of course, now it's just a regular camp. So much has changed in the last thirty-five years. It's kind of amazing."

"Yeah, it's not all roses and puppies of course, but you're right. A lot of progress has been made."

"I wish I … I mean, it's too bad that kid who died here couldn't live to see it."

Henry stared at Rick, this strange boy who sat still as a picture, and found his thoughts going off in strange and inexplicable directions. His imagination running rampant. He was about to say something when the alarm on his phone went off, startling them both.

"Unstructured exploration is over," Henry said, silencing the alarm. "Guess we need to get back."

"You go on," Rick said. "I can't go back. I can never go back."

Henry had already stood up, and he looked down at Rick with a frown. "They do roll call. Surely someone will miss you."

The sadness in Rick's eyes was profound and heartbreaking. "No one misses me. I don't think anyone even remembers me. But you should go. Your friends are waiting."

Henry hesitated. "I don't want to leave you here all alone."

"It's okay. Just talking to you helped. Really, it did. Thank you for that."

Still Henry didn't move. He felt the pull back to camp – the people, the voices, the laughter, the agenda of activities. Yet he also felt a pull to this lonely boy. After a minute, he crouched back down and planted a soft, tentative kiss on Rick's cold lips. When Henry pulled away, his own lips were numb and tingling.

Rick smiled, some of his sadness lifting like a shroud being removed. "Thank you for that, too. I never got kissed before."

Henry could think of nothing to say, so that was what he said. He rose again and started back toward the path. Just before he stepped onto it, he turned and glanced over his shoulder at the tree.

No one sat beneath it.

HERESY

God is dead.

I know people think gods can't die, but they can and they do. It takes a long time, millennia to eons, but everything living eventually perishes. It's a natural cycle that cannot be broken by even the most supernatural of beings.

Our god lasted longer than most. She walked the earth before humankind had slithered its way out of the ooze and muck, in the time of the giant beasts. In fact, she used to ride them like ponies and they were her first worshippers.

Of course, they disappointed her and in a fit of rage she obliterated them. Our god is powerful and awe-inspiring, but she has a temper and can be petty. She demands complete and unyielding devotion. Only the most faithful win her favor.

And only the most faithful of us are gathered now, for her funeral pyre.

I speak of her still in the present tense because though she has gone, I continue to feel her presence. Power like that can never truly be destroyed, not even in death. It only changes form and seeks another outlet.

Or outlets.

We number in the hundreds, dedicated worshippers but a paltry number compared to those who follow the modern gods. Perhaps that is what finally killed her, a lack of adoration siphoning away her life force. Speculation, but I feel honored to be among those who never faltered in my adulation and now I will get my recompense.

As the flames consume her glorious flesh, rendering it to ash and dust, the smoke churns into the sky like dark storm clouds, twisting and roiling and blotting out the sun. We hold hands and sing hymns long forgotten by the world, offering up prayers and benedictions. We have been here for nearly a day, not moving, ignoring our discomfort and exhaustion. We wait until the fire has died. Even now, we do not leave but only gather closer to the remains, despite the heat that still emanates from the smoldering embers.

The eldest priest among us gathers up the ash and charred bones and disperses them among us. Time has come for our last ritual, the final communion. We break apart, each taking a piece of our god, and then we consume her, take her into ourselves so that she lives inside us.

Some of us snort up her ashes; others boil down her blackened flesh and shoot it into their veins with needles; still others wrap her ashes in paper and smoked her. A few even break her bones open with hammers and suck out the marrow. The method does not matter, as the result is the same.

As soon as her ashes are inside me, a euphoria like none I've ever known grips me. I swoon, falling to my knees, as every inch of my skin begins to tingle with an almost electrical current. My eyelids flutter and my heart stutters in my chest. I feel sexually aroused and touch myself, sweat pouring from me despite the shivers that wrack my body.

I had always known being in the presence of our god was intoxicating, but now I see that all which had come before was merely a contact high. Actually having her inside me proves to be a more potent experience than I'd ever dreamed. I feel strong and beautiful, powerful and invulnerable. Like a giant in a world of Lilliputians.

I push shakily to my feet, knowing that this is a high that will not fade. I'll never crash from this, and as I look around me, I see all my fellow worshippers experiencing a similar revelation.

Only we are mere worshippers no more. We are changing, evolving, transforming. This is no mere high, but the ultimate high that can alter worlds and create new ones. The ritual is over, and this is our supreme reward.

Others begin to lift from the ground, freed from the restraints of gravity, and rise into the heavens. Off to find new worlds or make them, to dictate their own laws and religions, demand their own sacrifices and supplications. This is how gods reproduce, after all.

I linger a bit longer, watching the last of the embers and sparks fly away in the breeze like fireflies. I know that this too will be my ultimate fate, to give birth to new gods through my demise, but not for a very long time.

Finally, saying one last prayer of remembrance, I turn and ascend, off to explore and create and destroy. Will I be a benevolent deity or a tyrant? Will I inspire obedience through love or fear? I am excited to find out.

God is dead; long live the gods.

SEAN NICHOLS PACKS IT UP

Growling with frustration, Sean pushed away from the computer. The open document mocked him, the few lines of text serving only to accentuate the blank whiteness that took up the majority of the screen. The blinking cursor seemed to be challenging him, and it was a challenge he had failed to meet.

"What's wrong?"

Sean started and then laughed at himself. His wife, Janice, stood in the doorway, leaning against the jamb. "Nothing's wrong," he told her.

Jan glanced at the screen. "Writing not going well today?"

"There would actually have to *be* some writing for it to not go well. Mostly I've just been sitting here personifying the computer."

Jan crossed the room, bent and kissed Sean gently on the temple. "And what kind of personality does our computer have?"

"That of a bratty five-year-old, always sticking its tongue out at me and chanting, 'Na na na boo-boo.'"

"Hmm, sounds like the computer needs a timeout."

"Or I do. I just don't know; I'm beginning to wonder if it's all worth it."

A crease formed between Jan's eyebrows. "Wonder if *what's* all worth it?"

"All this time I've been investing in writing. Maybe I'm just kidding myself."

"Sean, you can't give up just because things didn't go well for one day."

"It's more than one day. When I was in college, I was convinced I would be a successful writer. It wasn't even a question, I just *knew* it. But I was stupid and thought it would all just fall into my lap, some kind of divine right or something. I wasted the years I should have really been busting my ass, and now look at me. I'm thirty-six and what do I have to show for all my dreams of success? A handful of published stories, mostly in small, unheard of magazines. By the time Stephen King was my age, he was in the midst of a best-selling career, and I haven't even been able to finish a novel in years."

"So what are you saying? You're just going to turn your back on the one thing you've ever been passionate about doing?"

Sean sighed, looking at the screen then quickly away, as if what he saw there hurt his eyes. "I used to be passionate about it, but I haven't really been feeling that for a while. Mostly these days it's a struggle to get anything done, and I'm never happy with the finished product. The last few stories I completed just feel...I don't know, *hollow*. Nothing comes out the way I envision it in my head, and it just doesn't seem worth all the effort. I just can't help but feel the time has come to stop living some kind of child's fantasy and face reality."

Jan ran her fingers through Sean's hair, smiling down at him. "I think maybe you just need a break."

"I'm sorry, I didn't mean to get so maudlin. It's probably just the stress from the upcoming move getting to me. You about to head over to the school?"

Jan nodded, suddenly looking very tired herself. "I still can't believe they're closing down the school. When I packed up my classroom, I thought for a minute I was going to cry."

"Save your tears. We haven't even begun to pack up the house yet."

"Don't remind me," Jan said with a groan. "Anyway, tonight some of us are going to start packing up the school library. You should come with."

"I don't know, I don't really feel up to seeing people."

"Come on, it'll do you good. Get your mind off things. Besides, there are a bunch of old books that were taken out of circulation that are up for grabs if anyone wants them."

Sean looked around at all the bookcases crammed with books that filled the room. "Well, the last thing I need is more books, but if they're free..."

"That's the spirit," Jan said, her lips blossoming into that wide smile that made her look just like the girl he'd fallen in love with years ago, the intervening years melted away in an instant. "Let's go."

***

"Mr. and Mrs. Nichols," Principal Herbert said. "Glad you could make it for our little Packing Party."

Besides Herbert, there were about a half dozen other teachers in the library, none of which Sean knew well. This was more Jan's crowd than his. He never felt entirely welcome among them, sensing that they disapproved of the fact that he only worked as a substitute teacher, Jan earning the majority of the money for the household so that Sean could have more time to concentrate on his writing. Even in the midst of the twenty-first century, there was still the prevailing prejudice that the man should bring home the metaphorical bacon.

Herbert smiled around the room and said, "Okay, I think this is everyone that's coming. We're going to start the arduous task of packing up the Reference section. Get ready to build up that upper body strength."

"Excuse me, I was thinking—" Sean began but stopped when all eyes turned to him.

Jan came to the rescue, as usual. "Actually, I sort of promised Sean he could pack up the out-of-circulation books and see if there was anything he wanted."

"I see," said Herbert, and his words were soaked to the saturation point in judgement.

Soaked to the saturation point in judgement. Sean thought for a moment that might be a good phrase to tuck away for use in a future story, but then he discarded it as stupid and overdone. Just the way he felt about most of the stuff he wrote these days.

"I don't have to," Sean said. "I can work in Reference with the rest of you."

"Don't be silly, Mr. Nichols." Herbert pointed to a pile of cardboard boxes. "Take a few of these; the out-of-circulation books are in the back storage room. Do you know where that is?"

Sean nodded. He had subbed for the librarian a few times.

"Good. Help yourself to whatever you want."

Jan gave him a quick peck on the cheek then she and the rest of the gathered teachers grabbed some boxes and headed for the Reference section. Sean stood for a moment, feeling more like an outsider than ever, then selected some boxes of his own and went into the storage room.

*** *

There were a lot more books than Sean had realized. He hadn't thought the school library large enough to contain this many discards, but he figured they'd been collecting back here for years. Most were dusty old hardcovers with spines so faded that the titles and author names were no longer legible, as well as stacks of paperbacks with torn covers and yellowed pages. The room smelled of old books, a spicy aroma that was impossible to describe but which Sean's nostrils recognized instantly.

The sight of all these unwanted books actually made him a little sad. They were like the homeless, no longer serving a purpose, abandoned and forgotten. Still, Sean would do his best to rescue as many as he could. He had already set aside several Bradbury books to take home with him. As Bradbury was one of his favorite writers, he actually already owned copies of these books, but he still felt the need to save them. Besides, he could probably send some of them to a friend of his in South Carolina.

Sean squatted down so he could reach the bottom shelf of a rusty metal bookcase. He gathered up an armful of books, which smelled as if they had begun to molder, and dumped them into one of the boxes. As he reached for more, he discovered that there was a second row of books behind the front one. He was surprised to note that the books tucked away at the back of the shelf appeared to be brand new, in pristine condition. Why would they be among the discards pulled from circulation? Unless, of course, they were victims of censorship, removed from the library to appease overly sensitive and overly righteous parents.

Picking one of the new books at random and pulling it out, Sean at first thought his eyes must be playing tricks on him. He actually rubbed at them, something so cliché that he would never have had one of his fictional characters do it, but what he saw remained the same. The cover was a parody of one of those hardboiled mysteries from ages gone by, a square-jawed detective in a fedora with a cigarette planted between his lips. The title was *Jack Carmichael Unfiltered*. The author, Sean Nichols.

Jack Carmichael was a novel Sean had written a few years back, part parody/part homage to the kind of testosterone-driven mysteries of the forties and fifties. Once he had completed the novel, he'd put it aside and done nothing with it, never even revised it let alone submitted it to any publishers.

Sean started pawing more of the books from the back of the shelf, tossing aside the older ones up front and grabbing the new ones. Here was *Crestfallen*, a thriller he had written one summer just for fun. And even *With Friends Like These*, a silly little caper novel he'd penned in college for the sole purpose of amusing himself and his group of friends.

This was impossible. Only a handful of people had ever even read these books; they'd certainly never been published. It occurred to Sean that this was Jan's idea of a joke, that she'd had someone print up these fake covers and stuck them on other books. After all, it had been *her* idea for him to come and go through these out-of-circulation books in the first place.

Sean flipped open *The Crestfallen* to the first page and started to read the opening paragraph, mumbling the words as he went along, recognizing them all.

This was his novel, all right. He flipped through and read random passages, all of which he recognized as his own work. He checked the copyright pages of the three novels. The earliest copyright date was for *Jack Carmichael* for 2025, three years in the future.

Confused and with a growing sense of panic, feeling that the world had come loose of its axis and was spinning out of control through space, Sean grabbed more of the new books from the shelf. He recognized all the titles as ideas he had outlined, but none of these books were even *written* yet. The copyright dates were all in the future.

Sean did something else that was too cliché even for a character in a book: he pinched himself. He felt the pain sharp and real in his flesh. The storage room suddenly seemed too hot, and the air was thick as molasses, getting caught in his throat and threatening to choke him. He wondered for a second if he was going to faint, but instead he seemed to become hyperaware. Everything in the room stood out in exaggerated detail. The *hiss* of the air-conditioning unit spitting cooled air through the vents, the smell of the books underlain with the scent of his own sweat, the dazzling colors of the books laid out before him. Those impossible books.

With shaking hands, Sean collected the novels and tossed them into an empty box, using only the tips of his fingers to touch them, as if they might be tainted in some way. He then grabbed the box and burst out of the storage room, practically running through the maze of mostly-emptied shelves to the Reference section, calling Jan's name as he went.

"Sean, what's the matter?" Jan said, dropping a thick dictionary on the floor and hurrying to him, concern stamped on her face.

Sean shoved the box toward her. "Look at these."

Jan took the box and stared down into it for a moment. Sean kept waiting for her face to register shock and consternation, but instead she just looked back up at her husband and said, "What exactly am I supposed to be looking at?"

"The books. Don't you *see*?"

Jan reached into the box and pulled out a tattered hardcover, its dog-eared pages coming unglued from the spine. "It's a collection of Jane Austen, so what? I didn't think you were a fan."

Sean snatched the box back and looked inside. Gone were the new hardcover copies of his future novels, replaced by a half dozen or so Austen novels that were in various stages of falling apart.

"But no..." Sean said, looking up at his wife. "These weren't..."

"What is it, Sean? What did you think you saw?"

Everyone had gathered close. Sean thought he could detect a smug look on their faces that suggested they had always suspected he was a little crazy.

Sean considered again the possibility that it had been a dream but discarded it just as quickly. If he had dreamt the books then he would have to still be dreaming because he had not woken up yet. Perhaps a hallucination brought on by sleep deprivation; since learning of the school closing and having to find a place to live in a new city, he hadn't been sleeping well. Or possibly a nervous breakdown. He had been under a lot of stress lately, some of it self-administered. Or...

Or maybe it was something else entirely.

"I'm sorry, I've got to go," Sean said suddenly, handing the box off to Herbert.

Jan reached out and took Sean's arm. "Are you okay?"

"Yeah, I'm fine. I just need to go home."

"Why? Are you sick?"

"No, nothing like that. I just...I need to write."

Jan blinked and let her hand drop from his arm. "Really? Earlier you were ready to give it up."

"What can I say? Inspiration struck while I was back there. I want to get it down before I lose it."

"Oh, sure, go. I'll be home when we're done here."

Sean kissed Jan, ignored the stares of the others, and hurried out of the library.

***

Sitting in front of the computer, the glow washing across his face, he typed slowly, the quiet *click-click-click* of the keys coming in long-spaced intervals. It wasn't like in a novel where, after the revelation in the library, he would have come back and banged out several stories with effortless ease. It was still a struggle, but now Sean was beginning to think that was okay.

Maybe it wasn't supposed to be easy. Maybe anything in life that was worth something came with a bit of pain. Maybe the struggle actually made a person stronger. Quitting was the coward's way out, Sean now thought, and he didn't like to think of himself as a coward.

In addition to starting a new story, Sean had also opened the file for *Jack Carmichael*. It was well past time he polished that novel up and got it ready for submission. The story had a lot of potential.

When Jan came home an hour and a half later, Sean was still at the computer. The words were starting to flow more smoothly now as he relaxed into the process. He tried not to think too much about what he was writing, but instead just tried to get lost in the story, to allow the narrative to whisk him away. Easier said than done, but he thought it was starting to work.

Without saying anything, Jan placed the box with the Bradbury novels in it next to his desk. Sean paused long enough to kiss his wife, tell her he loved her, then he returned to work.

He was still at it when Jan went to bed later that night.

UNHOLY GHOST

W hen the priest heard someone enter the confessional on the other side of the thin wall, he suppressed a groan. He was tired, his legs ached, and only ten minutes remained for the appointed confessional time. He hoped for a little old lady whose only real sin was thinking ill of her children for not visiting more often. In and out with a couple of Hail Mary's. No fuss, no muss.

The priest silently chastised himself for such uncharitable thoughts, adding them to his own list of sins he would need to confess. The confessional was a sacred place, and he was here to intercede on behalf of his parishioners so they could receive absolution for the transgressions. A sacred duty. He would stay here as long as needed.

He heard the confessor settle in on the wooden bench, and through the mesh of the window he caught sight of what appeared to be a young man. Possibly even a teenager. Hard to tell for sure.

The priest waited, but then the silence stretched out to almost a minute. Concerned, he said, "Child?"

The shape through the mesh jerked as if being awakened. "Oh, sorry. I forgot I'm supposed to start things off. Um, let's see. How did it go? Bless me, Father, for I have sinned. That's right, isn't it?"

The priest frowned and leaned forward slightly. This didn't seem like his usual confession, and he found himself forgetting about the time and his stiff legs as a natural curiosity overcame him. He had to admit that while most of the confessions he heard were rote and predictable, sometimes he heard ones that interested and fascinated and sometimes even titillated him. He wasn't proud but suspected many priests felt the same. Therapists too. You can't hear people's deepest, darkest secrets day in and day out and always react with total emotional detachment.

"How long has it been since your last confession, child?" the priest prompted.

"Since never. I've never given my confession before."

"Are you a member of this parish?"

"Not exactly, but my family used to be. When I was a little kid. We moved out of town when I was seven, and we stopped going to church altogether shortly after that."

The priest squinted to see if he could make out any of the young man's features, see if he looked familiar, but the parish was large and many had come and gone in the twenty years since the priest had been assigned here.

"May the Lord be on your heart and mind so that you may make a true confession of your sins," the priest said, automatically falling into the ritual.

"I definitely have a lot on my heart and mind, Father. However, before I start giving you my laundry list of sins, may I ask a question?"

"Certainly."

"Can a ghost sin?"

The priest's frown deepened. "Excuse me?"

"I mean, once you're dead, do sins still count against you? Is there some kind of loophole there?"

The priest's fascination became tinged with a frost of fear. Was he in the presence of a madman? "You believe yourself to be a ghost?"

Soft laughter issued from the other side of the confessional. "Not literally, Father. I guess a better comparison would be a zombie, but again I don't mean that literally. What I'm saying is that I feel dead on the inside. I still get up, go to work, eat, but there's no emotion in it. I'm like a phantom, wandering among the living but not truly one of them. Like I'm not part of this world, merely haunting it."

"And how long have you felt this way, child?"

"My whole life. Almost as if I were born a ghost. I killed my mother, you see. I guess that's my first sin to list."

"You murdered her?"

"Involuntary manslaughter, I guess you could say. She died giving birth to me. It was a difficult delivery and the doctors couldn't stop the hemorrhaging. My father never let me forget that I killed her."

"That is not your fault. The Lord definitely does not blame you for this, and neither should you. Your father was wrong to tell you such things."

"I hate my father, Father. I guess that's sin number two if you're keeping score."

"Child, I can understand why you would harbor resentment toward your father for holding you responsible for your mother's death, but–"

"That's the least of his sins against me. From as early as I can remember, he did things to me."

"*Things?*" the priest asked, though he wasn't sure he wanted to know more.

"Started out with just touching, fondling, but quickly went beyond that. He said that a man had needs, and since my mother was gone I had to be the one to fill those needs. He said it was my duty."

The priest recoiled from the mesh opening in horror. Horror at the unspeakable story the young man had to tell, but also horror at the fact that it sounded oddly ... familiar.

"I buried my father last week," the man went on. "Oh, I didn't kill him, but I wish I had. Sin three maybe? At least two and a half. He died of cancer, ate him right up from the inside out. Seemed wicked painful, which makes me think maybe there is a God or some kind of divine justice after all. Anyway, on his deathbed he offered no apology to me, but he did offer his own confession. A confession about a confession. He told me that he had once told a priest about what he was doing to me. He even remembered the priest's name. He sat right here in this little box and told you everything. We moved shortly after that because he got nervous, afraid you'd report him. But you never told a soul, did you, Father?"

The priest felt a chill spread up his spine and branch out until his entire body felt engulfed in a blanket of ice. He stammered out a lame response, or excuse. "I ... um, well, you have to understand ... you see, the seal of the confessional is sacrosanct ... I can't ... that is to say, I'm forbidden from revealing ..."

"I understand, Father. Your beliefs tell you it is more important to keep the confidence of a monster than to save a child from harm. Seems like I'm not the only one in this box with sins to atone for, huh?"

The ice that encased the priest turned to fire, and he felt sweat dribbling down his face, dripping into his eyes and making them burn. His fear mixed with shame. He did remember this young man's father, more than ten years ago now. One can't forget a confession like that. He had been sickened and horrified and pleaded with the man to get help ...

but he had not broken the seal. He had not told anyone or made any real attempts to help the boy.

"I don't know if what I'm about to do is a sin or justice or what," the young man said. "All I know is that there are about to be two ghosts in this confessional."

The priest could not clearly make out the gun through the mesh, but he heard the distinctive *click* of the hammer being cocked.

THE ROAD OF MANY HUES

At the end of the rainbow lies a pot of gold.
At least, that's what the stories told.

Barnaby didn't believe in fairytales, myths, or urban legends. At least, that's what he told himself. Yet desperate times called for desperate measures, to coin a cliché. His life had fallen apart. His wife had left him, he only had limited supervised visitation with the kids, he lost his job, and the foreclosure paperwork on the house had come just yesterday.

What did Barnaby have to lose? Might as well cling to a dream, no matter how unlikely.

Follow the road of many hues,
But be prepared to pay your dues.

After the rainfall, Barnaby got in his beat-up Honda and began puttering through the streets of his neighborhood. It only took him a few moments to spot the rainbow, arcing across the sky on the west end of town near City Hall.

He made a beeline for it but reached a dead-end of sorts at the woods that bordered Lake Prosperity. Barnaby abandoned the car on the soft shoulder and went into the trees, the apex of the rainbow directly above him now. He ran blindly through the woods, realizing that his actions were insane.

But sanity was overrated. A longshot was better than no shot, surely.

The way to the treasure is fraught with peril,
Snares and deadfalls and wild beasts gone feral.

In the periodic breaks in the overhanging branches, Barnaby thought he detected the rainbow fading. He quickened his pace, knowing that if the rainbow disappeared before he reached the end, he would never find the pot of gold.

Not that he really believed there was a pot of gold to be found. Even in the grips of his madness, he recognized it as such. Madness. Which meant maybe he was saner than he thought. Crazy people weren't supposed to know they were crazy, after all.

All around him he heard scuttling movement, crackling twigs and rustling leaves, but also low growls and deep snarls. Animals tracking him just out of sight, no doubt trying to frighten him from his goal. He ignored this and continued on his way.

> *If against all odds you survive this quest,*
> *You'll be faced with your greatest challenge yet.*

It seemed to be getting darker in the woods, despite the fact that it was only a little past noon. Underneath the animal sounds, Barnaby detected a rhythmic pounding, like someone beating drums. Frightening as all this was, it also gave him hope that he was nearing his journey's end. His belief in the rational fell away like a shed snakeskin, and he suddenly felt like a kid again. Believing in magic and fairies and leprechauns and Santa Claus and Jesus and all of it.

He would find that pot of gold, and with his riches he would be able to afford a good rehab that would get him clean once and for all, save the house from foreclosure, prove himself a fit enough parent for joint custody of the kids, maybe even win Caroline back. The solution to all his problems waited at the end of the rainbow.

Yet he also knew it wouldn't be that simple. He would have to earn his reward, and up ahead he saw the shimmering rainbow terminating at a rotting, hollowed-out tree. Gold nuggets poured out of an opening at the base of the trunk, sparkling in the fading light like the precious gems they were.

Despite the answer to his prayers lying so close, Barnaby came to an abrupt halt when he saw the thing step in front of the tree, blocking his way.

> *The troll that acts as guardian to the prize must be beat,*
> *Yet all but the strongest will find this to be an impossible feat.*

The battle lasted hours, and at the end Barnaby lay broken in the dirt, oozing blood from the dozens of slashes the creature carved into him with its yellowed claws. Bruises covered his body like a patchwork, and he suspected a few ribs were broken as was his nose.

The creature stood over him, those wicked claws poised just above his throat. One swipe of its stubby arm and that would be it for Barnaby. Game over.

"Do you want to live?" the creature asked in a gravelly voice, its breath rank like rotting fish and excrement.

Barnaby was surprised by how quickly the answer came. "Yes, please."

With a nod, the creature retreated, resuming its sentinel stance in front of the tree. As Barnaby watched, the rainbow faded away completely and both the creature and the tree disappeared.

After several minutes to gather his strength, Barnaby pushed himself to his feet and shambled back to the car. He hadn't won the prize, but perhaps he had gained something even more valuable. His life needed to be put back together, and if he could face the creature, perhaps he could trek that long path to recovery without the gold. He wasn't typically a man prone to thoughts of a poetic nature, but just maybe the rainbow had led to some treasure within himself.

With that thought, he drove off into an uncertain but hopeful future.

Win or lose, those who survive through perseverance
May very well find the treasure that they hold dearest.

FIFTEEN MINUTES FAST

Chester was running late. Not really, considering that he routinely arrived at work 45 minutes early, but he was such a stickler for punctuality that if he arrived just half an hour early, he *felt* late. He liked to leave the house by 6:30 and it was already 6:45.

Tossing his briefcase onto the passenger's seat, he slid the key into the ignition with one hand while securing his seatbelt with the other. The engine purred to life and he quickly backed out of the drive. The radio was tuned in to the local adult contemporary station, WJAM, and he was singing along with Nora Jones when he glanced at the dashboard clock...

...and nearly had a coronary. The clock read 7:00. He checked his watch again, and it still read 6:45. Could his watch have stopped or was it running slow? He unclipped the cell phone from his belt and checked the time on it. 6:45...no, wait, just turned 6:46. Breathing a sigh of relief, he returned the phone to his belt and started toward the interstate.

He wasn't sure how his dashboard clock had gotten to be fifteen minutes fast; he was almost sure it'd had the correct time last night. In any case, he'd fix it later. For now he just wanted to get to work.

Traffic on the interstate wasn't too heavy at this hour. It had rained the night before, leaving the pavement damp but the newly risen sun was drying up most of it. Chester increased the radio's volume and got lost in the easy listening, slipping into that autopilot state most commuters were familiar with.

A Bonnie Raitt song ended and the morning DJs, Dillard and Kimbo, came on, chattering away about celebrity gossip and current events. It was just background noise to Chester, but he perked up when he heard mention of the interstate on which he was currently traveling.

"That's right," Dillard was saying. "You might want to avoid the interstate if at all possible this morning. A pretty bad accident has got southbound traffic at a standstill near exit 82."

Chester was traveling southbound, and exit 82 was coming up in just a few miles. He didn't any signs of congestion yet, but he let up on the gas pedal in anticipation of it. He cursed himself for not leaving earlier this morning; if he got stuck in a traffic jam, he'd really be late.

On the radio, Kimbo was continuing with the story. "According to our sources, at approximately 7:05 a Honda Accord ran off the road and crashed into an abutment, exploding on impact. An eighteen-wheeler that was behind the car slammed on brakes, jackknifed, and overturned, causing a pileup."

"We'll keep you apprised of any further developments in this story. The time now is 7:20 on Monday morning..."

Chester frowned. Something didn't make sense here, and he began to wonder if perhaps this was not a live broadcast but a repeat of an old, taped show. For one thing, exit 82 was coming up straight ahead and there was no traffic jam; the way was clear. Also, Dillard said the time was 7:20, which was what his dashboard clock read, but that time was wrong, was actually fifteen minutes fast. Which meant the actual time was...

...7:05...

Which is when they said the accident occurred.

Chester was reaching for the radio dial to change the station when his car hit a slick patch of pavement and started to slide. Panicked, he slammed on the brakes, but that only made the slide worse.

The eighteen-wheeler behind him laid on its horn, and Chester began screaming as his Honda Accord rocketed toward the abutment.

KNOWLEDGE IS POWER

Thomas was surprised to find Heaven was a giant library.

Actually, he was surprised to find himself in Heaven at all. He had never been a religious man, finding all faiths equally preposterous and based on nothing solid. He respected facts, things you could prove, which is what had led him to science at a young age. As an adult, he had spent his life working for a company that developed surgical implants for people with heart conditions. So he had done good in the world, but had professed no fealty to any particular deity. His understanding from the times his mother forced him to go to church as a child was that such a profession was necessary to gain entry to Heaven.

Thomas began to meander through the library, looking at all the titles. There seemed to be a bit of everything. Novels, biographies, philosophical treatises, dense scientific texts, histories. The library itself seemed to have no end, an eternity of knowledge.

He had thought himself alone, a private Paradise which suited him just fine, but in a small alcove he found a dapper gentleman in a blue suit, white hair done up in a pompadour, reclining in an easy chair, reading a thick book.

"Oh," the man said when he noticed Thomas. "I'm so sorry, I meant to greet you when you arrived, but I got so engrossed. That's the danger of good books."

"You were expecting me?" Thomas asked.

"Of course." The man stood, placing a felt bookmark in the book and leaving it on the chair. "I prepared this place just for you."

"So you're…I mean, are you…God?"

The man gave a sheepish nod, looking uncomfortable with the title. "I am."

"It's a pleasure to meet you," Thomas said, feeling like a fool but he wasn't sure what else to say to a God he never really believed existed.

The man waved off the comment. "Please, I'm the one glad to finally meet you face to face. You have been one of my most devoted disciples."

"I think you may have mistaken me for someone else. I never devoted my life to you."

"Yes, you did," the man said with a gentle smile. "You may not have realized it, but everything about the life you led was in service to me. I don't demand that service, like it is sometimes suggested, but I do appreciate it."

Thomas frowned, rubbing at his temples the way he did when faced with a difficult problem. "I'm confused. Are you the God of the Bible, the one who created the Garden of Eden, Adam and Eve, all that sort of thing?"

"Ah, Adam and Eve," the man said wistfully. "I remember them well, and our time in the Garden."

"Wait, you kicked them out of the Garden," Thomas said. "For eating the apple."

"I did no such thing. That was Jehovah, a minor deity and one a little too rash and a lot too egotistical."

"So if that wasn't you, but you were in the Garden with Adam and Eve, does that mean you're...Lucifer?"

The man laughed. "That impetuous imp. Heavens no."

"Well, if you weren't Jehovah and you weren't Lucifer, and you obviously weren't Adam or Eve, then who were you in the Garden."

The man sat in the chair again, taking up his book. "Dear Child, I was the apple."

BRICK AT THE STONEWALL

Phil didn't mean to kill the cop. He'd intended only to observe the Stonewall Riots, to use the time displacer he'd invented to witness an iconic part of LGBT history. However, he'd gotten caught up in the melee and smashed the brick over the cop's head.

Running into an alley, he'd used the displacer on his wrist—which looked like nothing more than a watch—to bring himself back to the present.

"Carl," he called out before noticing this bedroom was unfamiliar, not the one he had shared with his husband for the past three years.

"Did you say something?"

Phil turned to find a strange woman, a fat toddler on her hip, standing in the doorway. He'd never seen her before...and yet she was so familiar. He was about to ask who she was but then the name came. "Yolanda?"

"Dinner will be ready in ten," she said then walked away down the hall.

Phil felt his memories shifting, a new timeline paving over the old. Because of the murder of the police officer, the Stonewall Riots hadn't become the rallying cry for a new LGBT movement. Instead it had caused the community to become even more reviled. More strict laws, heightened bigotry. No progression to allow gays in the military, no marriage equality. No Ellen, no *Will & Grace*. Homosexuality was still a crime and mental illness, and Phil himself was deeply in the closet.

He had to go back and fix this before it was too late, but when he looked down his wrist was bare, and then he couldn't remember what he was looking for in the first place.

With a sigh he went to have dinner with his family before going out to the park to troll for anonymous dick in the public restroom.

HALLOWEEN SLASHER MARATHON

The three boys met outside the theater. The marquis above proclaimed "HALLOWEEN SLASHER MARATHON! HALLOWEEN (1978), FRIDAY THE 13TH 2 (1981), NIGHTMARE ON ELM STREET 3 (1987)! ONE NIGHT ONLY!"

Jake checked the time. "First movie should be about halfway done."

Eddie nodded. "Think this w-w-will work?"

"Absolutely, as long as we're all committed to our characters. Right, Paul?"

Paul was glancing anxiously back down the street at the storefronts decorated with cardboard pumpkin cutouts and plastic skeletons. In the distance, some kids in costume crossed the street, feet kicking through drifts of dried autumn leaves.

"Right, Paul?" Jake said again, more loudly this time.

"Huh? Oh yeah. It's going to be great."

The three walked into the theater's lobby. Brenda, who worked the ticket counter, smiled at them and waved. The three boys came to see a lot of movies at the Rialto, so the older couple who owned and ran the place knew them well. Most of the kids from their high school went to the multiplex at the Mall, but the three friends preferred the quiet Mom & Pop theater that inexplicably kept going. Although the boys knew business was tough and that Brenda and Pete were always in danger of having to close up shop.

Which was why Pete had jumped at the idea the boys presented.

"My boys!" Pete exclaimed, coming out from behind the concession counter and approaching them with his arms held out as if for a group hug. "I could kiss all three of you right on the lips!"

"I think we'll p-p-pass on that," Eddie said with a laugh.

Instead, Pete put his fingers to his lips and blew them all a kiss. "You boys were right about the marathon bringing them in. The theater is absolutely packed!"

"Completely sold out," Brenda added. "First time that has happened in longer than I care to remember."

"Glad to hear it," Jake said. "They aren't showing anything over at the mall but stupid comedies and action movies. I knew if you offered some classic scary movies for Halloween it would draw them in."

"It did indeed," Pete said, giggling like a small boy. "Drew your friends in like flies to honey."

"We should probably get ready," Paul said, shifting from one foot to the other.

"Of course. You can change in the Men's Room."

The three friends went into the restroom, which was empty, and shrugged out of the backpacks they wore, pulling out their costumes. They didn't bother to go into the stalls but changed out in the open in front of each other. They were more like brothers than friends, and they had no shame or secrets from one another.

Once they were in costume, they took a minute to examine their reflections in the long mirror that ran the length of the metal trough sink. For store-bought costumes, they didn't look half bad.

Jake, in his navy-blue coveralls and white expressionless mask, was the epitome of Michael Myers. Eddie had opted for Jason Voorhees' trademark hockey mask, despite the fact that Pete and Brenda were showing the second movie in that series when the character still had a sack over his head, but the retractable plastic machete completed the outfit. Paul's latex mask was surprisingly detailed and realistic in its burn scars, and the tattered red-and-green sweater and the glove with the long blades transformed him into Freddy Krueger. The only thing marring the illusion was the three backpacks the boys had put back on, but they contained other props they would need later.

"Pete thinks t-those assholes in the theater are our f-f-friends," Eddie said, speaking through the holes in the hockey mask.

Jake shook his rubber butcher knife, watching it wobble. "Yeah, well, who needs them? We got each other."

The three had met in junior high and bonded instantly over their respective statuses as outcasts and pariahs. Eddie's stutter, Paul's limp from a childhood injury, and Jake's chronic acne—these things singled them out, separated them from the herd, but there seemed to be something deeper, more intrinsic but indefinable, that made them the sacrificial scapegoats for their peers. Their clothes, their taste in music and comic books, their sense of humor ... it was all out of fashion and never in step with what was "in."

Fact was, if anyone at school had realized the slasher marathon was their idea, if anyone had seen them putting up the flyers, it would probably have ended up a bust. Kids refusing to come to the Rialto on principle, because The Three Fagateers as they were collectively called couldn't possibly have any cool ideas.

But tonight they were going to show their classmates how cool they could be. They would make their classmates see them in a different light.

"Okay," Jake said, his hot breath inside the mask making him sweat. "Let's do it!"

The three exited the restroom and Brenda and Pete both cheered their costumes.

"You boys look terrific," Pete said. "When you start running up and down the aisles between the movies, the kids are going to flip out."

"They won't get a good night's sleep for the rest of their lives," Paul said in a cackling voice, waving with his gloved hands, the blades clinking together.

Another boyish giggle from Pete. "Think I'll sneak in with you boys so I can watch the fun for myself."

The three friends exchanged a glance then Jake shrugged. "Suit yourself."

Pete led the way, opening the double doors into the theater barely enough to squeeze through. The boys followed. Inside the darkened theater, the flickering illumination from the screen providing the only ghostly illumination, Pete scurried to one back corner and the boys to the other. No one in the crowd seemed to notice.

"L-l-look," Eddie whispered, scanning the seats. "It's not just k-kids from school. There are p-p-people our parents' age."

"Not surprising," Jake said. "These movies were popular when they were teenagers. Probably nostalgic for them or something."

On the screen, Jamie Lee Curtis—long before she needed Activia to keep her regular—stood on a porch, banging on a door and screaming for the little boy inside to hurry as Michael Myers advanced slowly across the street. The kids from school reacted not with terror but with laughter, throwing popcorn at the screen and yelling out cracks about Curtis's clothes and hair. They didn't seem scared at all.

Though that would change soon.

"We really gonna do this?" Paul asked.

Jake clamped a hand on his shoulder. "You're not chickening out, are you?"

Paul looked out at the crowd, probably remembering every time one of these kids had beat him up, stolen his lunch money, threw his books in the toilet, and then he shook his head. "No, I'm good."

Eddie went over to the double doors and slid his machete through the handles. Jake tossed down his knife, and Paul discarded his glove. The three shared a group hug that looked sort of like a huddle out on the football field, then they unshouldered their packs, unzipped them, and pulled out the guns.

THE ALIEN

I thought that we would never change;
We'd remain frozen in time,
Trapped in amber.
The same at forty as we were at twenty.
Young, dumb, unafraid of danger.

I thought life would be an eternal adolescence,
long nights of conversations about art
mixed with copious amounts of drink and dance.
Like nomads we would follow our passions wherever they led,
Taking meaningless temp jobs just to pay the rent.

But our true vocation would always be freedom,
The freedom that comes from no commitments
And is rewarded with penniless abandon.
The world of 9 to 5 and suits and ties
was to us an alien world of the mindless automaton.

I had pledged my soul to be an artistic vagabond,
shirking all adult responsibility
in exchange for a perpetual youth of spirit.
I thought our whole group was in uniform agreement
That nonconformity was the virtue we held dearest.

But one by one we began to drop like proverbial flies,
gradual at first, but as time wore on
more of us falling by the wayside in this war called life.
Marriage, babies, jobs at a desk
began to carry my friends away from the nomad light.

No more long nights, no more conversations about art,
instead terse and dismissive texts
that said things like, "Sorry, I'm busy."
My friends let their passions wilt and die on the vine
while I drank and danced alone in what felt like a suddenly
empty city.

Now when I see them, they are little more than strangers,
somewhat vaguely familiar like character actors

where you recognize the faces but not the names.
And in the end it is I who has become the alien
by being the one who stubbornly refused to change.

WAR ON CHRISTMAS

Santa was bleeding from a dozen wounds, and he couldn't move his left arm. He lay in the ditch, breath wheezing in vaporous puffs like smoke signals. His wife was nearby, but she wasn't moving and didn't respond when he called her name. The snow around her as well as her white hair were streaked with red.

No children were going to be getting presents this Christmas, though that was the least of Santa's worries. He just couldn't figure out how everything had gone so wrong. For so long he'd ruled over his little Kingdom at the top of the world, his wife by his side, his workers making the toys he distributed to all the good children of the world. And then his workers had gone and ruined everything.

They rose up against him, said they were tired of being enslaved to him, working year-round with no compensation. Why, had they ever considered that Santa himself wasn't *paid* for the service he provided to the young ones? The payment was their joy on Christmas morning. The workers should have been happy to be a part of that.

Instead they had waged war. They were small, but they were many. Santa and his wife were no match for them. Even the reindeer had sided with them. All except for Rudolph. He had never forgotten how the other reindeer had initially shunned him, calling him a freak for his unusual nose. Santa was the one who had realized what an asset that nose could be, and Rudolph remained loyal.

Even in the face of inevitable defeat.

Santa called the deer over now, his nose shining like a beacon. Rudolph had suffered his own wounds, but he dragged himself to Santa's side.

"Rudy, I'm afraid I'm not long for this world," he said, bloody spittle flying from his lips. "I fear I have only moments left. I want you to go to the others, surrender, ask to join them."

Rudolph shook his head vehemently.

"Yes, Rudy, do this for me. My last request. I want you to show remorse, convince them you are sorry and want to be a part of their community again. You need to really sell it so they will welcome you in. And then you will deliver one last present for me. A present for all those ungrateful little bastards."

With the last of his strength, he raised his right arm. Rudolph hesitated then took the grenade.

FAMILY REUNION

"We shouldn't be out here," eight-year-old Derek said. "Aunt Teresa will be furious if she finds out."

Derek's twelve-year-old brother Ronald gave him an annoyed look. "She's not going to find out. As far as she knows, we're out trick-or-treating."

The two were in costume, Derek dressed as a pirate and Ronald as a zombie, and both had floral-patterned pillowcases they'd taken to ostensibly collect candy but had actually used to sneak out supplies they'd need for the ritual.

Now they sat in the dewy grass at the back end of Mountain View Cemetery well past dark, their faces lit by the wavering illumination of thirteen black candles placed in a circle around themselves and the double tombstone of their parents, killed six months ago in an automobile accident. In the nearby neighborhoods they could hear the sounds of children laughing as they went door to door, begging for treats, but it seemed very distant, like alien noises from another world.

"Are you sure this will work?" Derek asked. "Where did you even find this spell?"

"On the internet," Ronald said, digging around in his pillowcase. "Seems pretty legit as far as resurrection spells go. All you need is the night of All Hallows Eve, the candle placement, and the incantation."

Derek clutched his own pillowcase to his chest like a security blanket. "And then just like that, our parents will be returned to us?"

"Not exactly. There's one more ingredient we'll need for the ritual to work."

"What's that?"

Ronald turned to his brother, pulling the butcher knife out of his pillowcase. "The sacrifice of a blood relative. Sorry, little brother, but if it's a trade of you for Mom and Dad, there's really no choice."

"I know," Derek said, moving before his older brother could. He'd brought a steak knife, and he lunged forward, ramming it into Ronald's throat, into the soft spot just below the Adam's apple.

The wide-eyed look of surprise on Ronald's face would have been comical under other circumstances, and he tried to speak or scream but all that came out was a high-pitched whistling as blood sputtered from his lips, almost indistinguishable from all the fake gore that covered him as part of his costume. He toppled forward and landed on top of his parents' grave.

Derek stared down at his brother, a half-smile twitching at his lips as Ronald's blood seeped into the earth, trailing down like roots to find their parents. "Sorry, big brother," Derek said. "But you're not the only one who can look stuff up on the internet."

THE TOOTH

arl found the tooth in a trunk full of Edward's things.

Edward had been gone almost four months, and Carl had finally felt strong enough to go through his belongings. Not his clothes or important papers or books or toiletries. Not anything he had used on a daily basis, not anything that *mattered*.

No, Carl had decided to start with this trunk in the basement, full of detritus, things you keep for sentimental reasons but which stay packed away and rarely looked at. Not the true mementos of a life, but the clutter.

Two cardboard boxes sat nearby, one marked "KEEP" and the other "DISCARD." Carl lifted the trunk's lid, a musty aroma of mildew and age tickling his nose. He closed his eyes, took a deep breath, then began rummaging through the items.

Old bowling trophies from high school. Yearbooks. Some moldering children's books saved from Edward's boyhood days. Birthday and Christmas cards. An ivory/ebony chess set. Each of these items Carl lifted from the trunk and placed in the "KEEP" box.

Which was ridiculous, he knew. If he wasn't going to throw anything out, he might as well keep it all in the trunk. It was simply too hard to part with anything that had belonged to Edward. It might have been different if he'd had the closure that comes from a funeral and a grave to visit, but Carl had been cheated out of all of that.

It was their own fault, really, Carl's and Edward's. If they'd simply tied the knot, made their relationship legal, then Edward's parents couldn't have cut Carl out the way they had. But they hadn't. They'd first become a couple back in 1991, long before gay marriage was legal anywhere in the country, and by the time it was, they had been together so long it hardly seemed necessary.

Besides, Edward had often said, marriage was an institution made up by straight people, a club they didn't let gay folks in for centuries, and now that they had reluctantly opened the doors, Edward wasn't so inclined to join.

Carl had thought the reasoning rather silly, but he'd gone along. Their love had been just as real in all the years before marriage equality; they didn't need a piece of paper to validate it. Making their relationship legal hadn't seemed important.

Of course, now Carl realized just how important that piece of paper was, and how not having it could erase a lifetime together as if those years never existed.

When Edward died, as far as the law was concerned, Carl was a legal stranger to the man. They hadn't even had power of attorney for one another. Therefore, Edward's body and funereal plans were handed over to his next of kin, his parents, despite the fact Mr. and Mrs. Foster had cut their son out of their lives decades ago.

Carl had heard from a sympathetic cousin of Edward's that the Fosters had their son cremated and kept the ashes. For all Carl knew, they had scattered them in some churchyard so that their son could be sanctified from his evil ways in death.

Doesn't matter, Carl tried to tell himself for the hundredth time. *Those ashes were not Edward. You still carry the* real *Edward around inside you. He exists in your memories of the years you spent together, the objects he left behind. His parents can't touch that.*

He knew this was the truth, and yet he also knew that the memories felt hollow, the things left around the house mere movie props. He would have given anything to be able to sit by a tombstone, to reach out and trace the letters of Edward's name, leaving flowers and wreaths and little mementos. It was part of the grieving process, part of the healing process, and being denied that meant the wound never scabbed completely over.

Musing on these matters, the pain filling him up like jagged glass, Carl lifted a tattered blanket that Edward had carried around as a child (he'd said he called it his "woobie" for some unknown reason) and saw a small beige box had been hidden underneath. The size of a ring box. Pausing to sniff the blanket, getting not Edward's distinctive scent but only a noseful of stale mildew, he tossed it with the other items to "KEEP" and picked up the small box, figuring inside would be Edward's high school ring.

Yet when he popped open the box, he found something quite different and quite unexpected.

Sitting on a bed of satin under a plastic bubble was a tooth. On the inside of the box's cover, printed in cursive script, were the words, "Eddie's 1st Baby Tooth."

Carl wasn't aware that he'd started crying until the first few teardrops dribbled off his chin and splattered on his arm. He tore off the plastic and upended the box so that the tiny tooth dropped into his palm. Closing his fingers, he gripped the tooth in his fist like a pebble and placed the fist against his lips.

The tears came in a torrent now, accompanied by huge wracking sobs. This tooth had once been a part of Edward, it contained his DNA, the only concrete part of the man that Carl had left.

With a shuddering breath, he pushed to his feet and made his way up the stairs into the kitchen then out the sliding glass patio doors and into the backyard. Dusk was settling like fine ash, a blaze of light to his left the final dying declaration of the day. At the very back of the property, by the plank fence, was a small patch of ground that Edward had used for compost. Each day he buried scraps of uneaten food and coffee grounds and eggshells, creating a dark and fertile soil in which Edward had intended to plant a garden.

Of course, he'd been intended to do that for the last two years of his life. He'd never gotten around to it, despite his commitment to composting.

Now Carl dropped to his knees and reached for the garden trowel that still stuck in the dirt at the edge of the compost pile where Edward had last left it, probably the night before the car accident that took his life. Carl certainly hadn't touched it since.

At least, not until now.

He dug a small hole then dropped the baby tooth into the crater and covered it over with fragrant earth. He then planted the trowel right on top of that, a makeshift marker that would have to do until he could find something more permanent. He hustled over to the magnolia tree that grew in the corner of the yard, its branches overhanging the fence, and picked up a few of the blossoms that had fallen to the ground. These he placed around the trowel.

"Now I have a grave to visit," he said, feeling silly and yet not at the same time. Carl had been an agnostic leaning toward full atheism since he was a teenager, so he didn't really believe that Edward could hear him, but that didn't matter. This was about Carl, what he needed. Edward had been taken so suddenly that Carl had been cheated out of any chance to say goodbye, so he would take whatever opportunity he could get.

"I love you," he said softly, the rhythmic chirruping of crickets lending a gentle music to the night and the strobe of fireflies a romantic light. "And I miss you so much I can't stand it, so much that some days I don't know how I'm going to go on without you. But I know you would want me to go on, and I'm going to try. It's not easy, though. I feel like I'm missing a piece of me, that I'm only half a man. I don't think I'll ever be whole again."

Carl put his fingers to his lips then reached out and patted the ground where he'd buried the tooth. Then he sighed and wiped the tear streaks from his face before standing and going back inside the house.

***

Around midnight, Carl finally cried himself to sleep. Not just because of the impromptu memorial service he'd held in the backyard, but because this had become his normal routine over the past four months. He could white-knuckle his way through most days, but lying in bed in the dark left him defenseless against the anguish and the emptiness.

His sleep was thin and filled with nightmares. Tonight he dreamed that he was in a cavernous, labyrinthine library, searching for a specific title that eluded him. Thousands of books surrounded him, perhaps millions, the entirety of the world's literature except the one book he sought. He kept returning to the old-fashioned card catalogue, pawing through the narrow drawers, and then returning to the stacks, continuing his endless, fruitless search. Finally, atop the highest shelf accessible only by a ladder, he found the object of his quest, but when he opened the book, he discovered all the pages were blank.

With a strangled cry, he jerked awake. Lying on his side, his pillow damp from his tears, he reached over to the bedside table for his cell to check the time. 2:47 a.m. Despite the scant time he'd spent asleep, he suspected there would be no more rest tonight. He considered getting up, trying to find something on TV or even reading a book, something to occupy his mind so he didn't spend the next several hours staring into the shadows and falling further into despair.

Yet he couldn't seem to muster the energy to climb out from underneath the covers, so he lowered his head back to the pillow. He wasn't sure how long he laid that way, eyes locked at the far corner but really looking inward where an internal projector played home movies of memories once sweet like cream and sugar but not tainted with a bitterness like black coffee, when he felt the mattress shift beneath him, a distribution of weight as if someone had climbed onto the bed.

Carl's entire body went rigid, and he found himself holding his breath. The sensation was so familiar. He'd often turned in before Edward, and he would feel that slight jostling when the other man finally crawled under the covers. He'd once mused that it was a homey feeling, a feeling of companionship and closeness. Until this minute, he hadn't realized how much he'd missed that feeling.

Which was why he must have imagined it now. Because it had to be his imagination, no other explanation for it. His mind reaching out through his pain and conjuring up a little cold comfort.

Even as he thought this, the mattress shifted again and he heard the springs squeak faintly. At the same time, his nostrils filled with the rich, verdant smell of freshly turned earth. A smell that encompassed life and growth and renewal. Carl had smelled it earlier when he'd buried the tooth.

Planted the tooth.

Underneath the earthy smell was another, less definable but instantly known to Carl. It was the distinctive smell that had been unique to Edward. His sweat, his natural scent, his Cool Water cologne...all combined and mingled into a single aroma that defined the very essence of Edward.

"Eddie?" Carl said, his voice quaking, as he rolled over, expecting to find the left side of the bed as empty as it had been since Edward's death, a vast plain of nothingness that mirrored the nothingness Carl felt inside.

He sucked in a gasp when he saw instead Edward lying there, his body outlined in silver highlights from the moonbeams filtering through the window. He was naked, smears of dirt painting his body in places. His face was obscured in shadow except for the shine of his eyes and teeth as he smiled.

Carl leaned up on his elbows, his breath catching in his throat like a dry piece of bread. This was a dream, it *had* to be a dream, but if it was, it was the best dream he'd had in months and one he didn't want to wake from.

Edward moved forward and wrapped his arms around Carl, and Carl melted into the embrace. Their lips met, and in that contact was fire and electricity and hunger. Like their first kiss all those many years ago. Carl surrender to the sensation, no longer caring if this was a dream or reality. That seemed unimportant; all that mattered was being in his love's arms once again and feeling Edward's firm body pressed again his own.

They fell back into the bed, Edward on top, tongues thrusting, hands exploring, heat rising. Carl could feel his lover's hardness and his own body responded in kind. It took only seconds for him to slip out of his boxer-briefs and kick them aside so that naked flesh rubbed against naked flesh, creating enough friction to spark a flame.

When Edward entered him with that old familiar blend of pleasure and pain, Carl hissed air in through his teeth and locked his arms around Edward's neck. "I miss you so much," he said between desperate kisses. "I'm just a shell without you. I need you to fill me up."

"I'm always with you," Edward replied, breathing the words into Carl's mouth. "*Always*. Death can take my body, but not my soul, and my soul is joined with yours. Never forget that. Anytime you feel lonely, just close your eyes and *feel* me instead."

The lovemaking was frantic and ferocious, as it always had been. As if they had not merely a physical need for contact but an emotional imperative to join their bodies as one, forming some kind of Siamese hybrid. Carl closed his eyes and bit his lip and lost himself in the feeling of surrender, the smell of sweat and passion, the sounds of the moans and grunts, the taste of Edward's tongue. His body seemed to melt away until he was nothing but his senses, a being not of corporeal form but untethered sensation.

Edward let loose a throaty, hoarse groan and then emptied himself inside Carl. Carl let loose a cry of his own, a sound of unrestrained joy, as he felt himself being filled. He clutched Edward close to them, the sweat of their chests binding their flesh like glue. He whispered "I love you, I love you," over and over as Edward pulled out and rolled onto his back, the two of them settling into their customary configuration. Edward on his back, Carl cuddled up to his side with his head on Edward's shoulder.

Carl's left hand continued to stray over Edward's body, exploring the curves and contours, the areas of hardness that gave onto areas of softness. Part of him knew this wasn't real, could only be a dream, unconscious wish fulfillment, but he could live with that. At least for now.

Feeling warm and secure, Carl began to drift off. The last thing he heard before falling asleep was Edward's voice saying, "I'll love you for all time."

***

Carl awoke the next morning feeling sore but content. He stretched and reached out for his phone. 7:32 a.m. He'd overslept, only 28 minutes before he was supposed to be at work, but he made no move to get up. He lay in bed, staring up at the ceiling, replaying last night's dream in his mind. It had been so vivid, so sensory and immersive. The details did not fade as dreams often did upon waking, but remained as vibrant and powerful as they had in the midst of the fantasy. Even the happiness he'd felt in the dream lingered, whereas he would have expected to be crushed to awaken to a world without Edward once again.

After making a quick call to the office to tell them he wouldn't be in until after lunch, he finally sat up in bed. That was when he noticed that the coverlet was caked with dirt. Pushing back the covers, he found even more dirt, and his own naked body was tattooed with streaks of mud. His underwear was tangled in the sheets at his feet.

Carl leapt out of bed, nearly falling face first to the floor in his haste, grabbing a robe from a hook on the back of the closet door, and hurried through the house, into the kitchen and out the patio doors. Halfway across the yard, he could see that the compost pile where he'd buried the tooth the night before had been disturbed. The dark soil was sprayed all over the grass as if something had erupted from the ground, leaving behind a crater as big around as a manhole cover and several feet deep.

Carl stood at the compost pile, staring down into the dark hole. His breathing came rapid and shallow, and he realized he was on the verge of hyperventilating. He began to turn in a slow circle and called out, "Edward! Edward, where are you?"

But of course he knew. Edward had been uprooted, and nothing uprooted could survive for very long. Not unless it was replanted elsewhere.

Placing his hands over his pounding heart, Carl began to cry. He realized Edward had been replanted, had planted his seed inside of Carl. Carl felt a warmth smoldering in his chest, like a furnace behind his ribcage, and it seemed to grow and expand throughout his entire body. He no longer felt incomplete or empty. He felt *whole*.

A slight smile curling his lips, hands still clasped above his heart, Carl turned and walked back to the house.

IN A WHIRLWIND OF AUTUMN LEAVES

"**D**addy, come on!"

Billy's father stood on the sidewalk at the corner of Jefferies and Laurel, staring down at the cellphone in his hands. Billy tugged at the man's jacket.

"Just a minute," his father said without looking up from the small screen. "I'm in the middle of something."

Billy groaned behind the rubber mask that turned him into green warty goblin. The brown poncho he wore to round out his costume was heavy, and despite the chill October wind that sent the crisp autumn leaves scurrying across the pavement, he was sweating.

Not that he minded. It was Halloween, and he'd endure any number of discomforts for the prospect of CANDY CANDY CANDY! It was the night of the year he anticipated more than any other, with the exception of Christmas Eve. He'd picked out this costume mid-September, and he'd been dreaming of trick-or-treating ever since the first leaf had turned yellow-orange on the maple in the front yard.

Typically, his mother took him out on Halloween night, but this year she was feeling a bit under the weather, so his father had volunteered. Which would have been fine if his father wasn't constantly distracted by his phone.

They'd been out for half an hour and had only made it one block.

Billy watched in dismay as a host of short monsters paraded by. Ghosts, vampires, zombies, witches. All accompanied by adults who were smiling as they held their kids' hands and led them from one house to another.

"Daaaaddyyyy!" Billy said, stomping his foot on the cement. "Everybody's gonna be out of candy by the time we get there."

With a sigh, Billy's father tore his gaze from the phone long enough to glance down at his son. "Have a little patience, Billy boy! I'm having a bit of a work crisis, and I need to get some stuff taken care of."

"But Daddy, it's Halloween."

"My bosses don't care about Halloween. I'll tell you what, you just run along and go to all the houses on this side of the street while I finish up this email."

"By myself?" Billy said, feeling a shiver run up and down his spine. At 9 years old, he considered himself a Big Boy, but the prospect of wandering the neighborhood at night on his own frightened him.

"Just to the end of the block, about four houses. Once you reach the next intersection, you come on back here. I should be finished by then."

Billy turned his head to stare down Jefferies Street to where it intersected with Wilkinson. Just one city block, but it seemed to stretch on for miles. Yet the fear of being away from his father's side in the dark was eclipsed by his desire for the candy he knew waited behind the doors of these houses. Besides, there were plenty of streetlamps and porch lights keeping the shadows at bay.

"Promise you'll be right here?" he asked, only a slight quaver to his voice.

"Count on it, Billy boy," his father said, his attention already returned to the phone.

Steeling himself with a deep breath, which filled the inside of the mask like a warm vapor, Billy left his father's side and started slowly down the sidewalk to the first house. A gaggle of children were coming back down the walkway, giggling and peering into their bags and plastic jack-o'-lantern buckets at the candy they'd just scored.

Billy made his way to the porch alone. On the top step an animatronic crow turned its head, flashed red eyes at him, and let loose with a mechanical caw. A cellophane witch was plastered on the large front window next to the door. Billy rang the bell and waited, clutching his orange and black bag like a security blanket. He called out a tentative "Trick or treat" as the door opened.

An old lady with a billowy white could of hair and cats-eye glasses stood before him, oohing and aahing over his costume as she deposited several fun-sized candy bars into his sack. He saw a Mounds, which wasn't his favorite, but also a Snickers and Milky Way which he loved.

Bolstered by the promise of more chocolatey goodness, he went to the next three houses with enthusiasm, no longer worried about being away from his father's side. In fact, he ceased to think about his father at all, and never looked back to make sure the man was still waiting on the corner. He bounded from door to door, his "Trick or treat" becoming more enthusiastic and boisterous each time. At the end of the block, he finally glanced back down Jefferies. His father was spotlighted under a lamppost, still tapping away at the phone, not even looking in Billy's direction.

Billy stood there for a moment, rocking back and forth on the balls of his feet. He had always been an obedient child, never getting up to any serious mischief, and he rarely defied his parents' instructions.

But what harm could come from him crossing Wilkinson and continuing down the next block? It too was well lit, with plenty of other kids and their parents going house to house. If he waited on his father, it could take them fifteen minutes to get down the one block when Billy could do it in five on his own? He'd be careful, checking both ways before crossing the street, then at the end of the block he'd cross to the other side of Jefferies and make his way back. Immersed as his father was in his work email, he likely wouldn't even notice Billy had strayed farther than he'd been told to go.

Deciding to break the rules for once, Billy checked for traffic then crossed the street. The wind gusted, sending a flurry of leaves into his path as if trying to stop him. He kicked through them, laughing and enjoying the scritch-scratch sound they made.

At the first house on this new block, he got a large bag of M&Ms and a box of cracker jacks. Walking back to the sidewalk, his head was down as he peered into his bag, looking at all his sugary loot. The wind rose again with a keening howl, sounding like something in pain, and the leaves were lifted up into a whirlwind that encircled him like the cyclone in *The Wizard of Oz.* The brittle leaves scratched at his poncho and scraped along the rubber mask, and they spun around him in such great numbers that they blocked out his vision with a blurring kaleidoscope of orange, red, and brown.

Billy, initially delighted by the sensation of being caught in the middle of this gaily painted whirlwind, began to feel frightened. He stumbled forward, flailing and kicking out at the leaves, then stumbled and fell down hard on the pavement. The impact caused him to bite his tongue, and pain flared even as the coppery taste of his own blood filled his mouth.

The cyclone of leaves had finally torn apart, the various pieces skittering away into the night like scurrying insects. Billy stood slowly, rubbing at his bruised tailbone. He bent to retrieve his dropped trick-or-treat sack then straightened his mask which had gotten knocked askew in the fall.

Only then did the boy register that the street had grown dimmer. Looking up at the streetlamps, he saw that several of them had gone out, and those that still glowed gave off only a sickly yellow light that served to accentuate the darkness instead of alleviating it. There were no longer any porch lights shining like beacons. The wind changed directly suddenly, and all those leaves that had skittered away before now came back his way, as if giving chase. Billy glanced down Jefferies Street, back the way he'd come, hoping to catch a glimpse of his father. All he saw that way was a wall of shadow that looked as solid as cement. He was afraid if he walked into the darkness, he would be swallowed whole and never seen again.

"Daddy?" he called out in a tiny voice that seemed not to carry any further than the tip of his nose. "Daddy, are you still there?"

There was no response. In fact, the night was utterly still and quiet except for the rustling leaves. All the other trick-or-treaters and their parents seemed to have fled. As much as the darkness scared him, being out here alone scared him even more. He started shuffling back toward Wilkinson. The houses looked different shrouded in shadow, more sinister and they seemed to lean at odd angles as if set on crooked foundations. The pavement as he crossed the intersection was cracked and broken where he remembered it being smooth before.

The sound of the leaves now resembled laughter, the mean-spirited tittering of a witch as she bakes small children in her oven. Billy picked up his pace, not quite running but definitely more than a walk. Maybe a trot.

He had nearly reached the end of this block and there was no sign of his father. He'd been waiting on the corner the last Billy had seen of him, but now the sidewalk was deserted. Billy stood there, eyes desperately scanning the area. He sensed movement at the house next to him, and he turned just in time to see what he had thought was an animatronic crow before flap its wings and take flight, buzzing past Billy's face so closely that feathers beat against the mask.

"Daddy!" Billy shouted, feeling tears sliding down his cheeks. He crouched down on his haunches with his back to the splintering lamppost and gave in to a fit of sobbing like he hadn't done since he was in diapers. Why would his father have left him? Was it like in that story his mother told him at bedtime a few weeks ago, *Hansel and Gretel*. The idea that parents would abandon their children had terrified him, and now he was living it.

"Are you okay?"

Billy looked up at the sound of the voice to see a group approaching him from down Laurel Street, a group comprised of three kids and two adults. A familiar enough tableau on Halloween night, but there was something about these people that seemed a bit off. It took Billy a moment to realize what it was.

The parents were in costume and the children were not.

Although as they came closer, stopping just in front of him, he realized that wasn't true. The kids were in costume, but the adults' costumes were so much more elaborate and horrific. The children were dressed as a baseball player, a mailman, and a cheerleader respectively. The father was done up as a werewolf, with a very convincing furry mask with yellow eyes and snarling teeth, hairy arms and legs jutting out of ripped clothes. The mother looked like a giant insect of some kind, covered in hard body armor with wiggling antennae and multiple arms. It was an impressive costume, and Billy couldn't even begin to fathom how she'd gotten herself into it. The spectacle of the two adults' costumes temporarily took his mind off his troubles.

"Why are you crying?" asked the little cheerleader, bringing Billy crashing back down to reality.

"I can't find my Daddy."

The insect lady said, her voice clipped and high-pitched, "Are you lost, little one?"

"No, I'm not lost. My Daddy is lost. He was right here and now he's not, and I don't know where to find him."

The werewolf got down on one knee so he was at Billy's eye level. This close-up the mask was even more impressive, and the breath that wafted from the snout had the slightly sour smell of meat on the verge of going bad. "Do you live around here?" he asked in a growly voice.

Billy looked around at his surroundings, feeling like he had stepped into a nightmare. He should know this neighborhood, he'd ridden his bike along the streets all last summer, and yet nothing looked familiar to him now. He couldn't even find any of the landmarks that usually helped orient him.

Where was the white-picket fence in front of the Haversham's house, or the Stevens' tacky lawn ornaments? The towering oak tree with the tire swing hanging from one of the lower branches should have been just across the street...except it wasn't. He should know exactly where he was, but he may as well have been on another planet. This sense of disorientation only led to more tears.

"Oh dear," said the insect lady, reaching out with one of her multi-jointed arms to pat him on the shoulder. "I'm sure your father will turn up soon. We'll wait with you until he does."

"But Mom," whined the mailman, "I want more treats."

The werewolf swatted the boy gently on the back of the head. "Show a little compassion. This boy is lost."

"He can come with us," the baseball player said.

The insect lady shook her head. "He should stay put in case his father returns." Turning her wide black eyes back to Billy, she quickly added, "*When*! I mean *when* your father returns."

"He can come with us," said the cheerleader. "We'll just go to the houses on the other side of the street. That's still in the area."

"I don't know."

Billy sniffled and said, "I wouldn't mind." He was still scared, but less so now that there were other adults present. Nothing too bad could happen with adults present. Besides, he still wanted to fill his sack.

The other three children cheered and clapped and the werewolf said, "Okay, fine, but just the houses across the street."

The two adults let the four children across Jefferies Street and up to the first house. Not only were the oak and tire swing gone, but Billy could have sworn this house used to be red brick instead of rough gray stone.

At the door, a big slab of wood twice as tall as a normal door, the werewolf lifted a heavy brass knocker shaped like a bat and let it fall against the wood with a hollow *thud*! Then the two adults stepped back and left the children to stand before the door with their sacks held out.

The door opened with a pronounced creak, and the tallest person Billy had ever seen stepped over the threshold. Draped in a brown robe, the hood of which completely concealed the face, skeletal hands sticking out of the sleeves, one of which gripped a scythe with a gleaming blade. An impressive Grim Reaper costume. Billy wondered if perhaps the person was on stilts under the robe, but the size of the door suggested otherwise.

"Trick or treat," Billy called out in unison with the other three children, although it sounded oddly as if the baseball player, the mailman, and the cheerleader said, "Tricks *are* treats."

The Reaper reached the free hand into one of the many folds in the robe and then started dropping items into each sack. The hand went so deep in each bag that Billy couldn't see what kind of candies they were getting. Then the Reaper seemed to float back into the house, the door slamming shut in the children's faces.

Going back down the walk, the other there were chattering excitedly as they glanced into their bags. Billy scanned the street again for his father then looked into his own bag, expecting to find peanut butter cups or marshmallow pumpkins or candy corns...

...but what he saw instead caused him to yelp like a kicked dog and drop his bag. Out spilled all the candy he'd collected so far tonight, as well as the fat slimy worms that the Reaper had apparently just given him.

"Eww," said the cheerleader. "Who put that gross stuff in there along with the goodies?"

Billy pointed back at the house they'd just come from. "He had to have done it, I know these weren't in my bag before. You guys didn't get the same?"

They all peered back in their sacks and shook their heads.

"Why would anyone play such a vicious prank on a child?" the alien lady said.

"Maybe it's because you're not wearing a costume," the cheerleader said to Billy.

The boy frowned inside his mask. "What are you talking about?"

"Well, it's Halloween. You're supposed to dress up, not just come out as you are."

Billy bristled at this, assuming the girl was making fun of him. "Hey, that's not very nice."

"She's got a point," the mailman chimed in. "Couldn't your folks afford to get you a costume?"

"This is my costume, you bunch of jokesters," Billy said then reached up and pulled the rubber goblin mask off his head.

The three children screamed and started backpedaling away from him. At first he thought this was just more of their cruel mockery, but then he saw that the werewolf and alien lady were reacting the same. Surely adults wouldn't be so mean.

The baseball player bumped into the mailman who in turn bumped into the cheerleader. Their bags fell open, spilling out tangled mounds of worms and snails and snakes and toads. All three children toppled to the ground like dominos, and that was when their faces fell off.

Not their real faces, but the masks they wore.

Under the baseball player mask was an alien head that was a smaller replica of his mother's; the mailman façade fell away to reveal a furry werewolf head; the cheerleader's real countenance was so misshapen and foreign and hideous that Billy's mind could barely comprehend it.

Now it was Billy who screamed and backpedaled. He fell onto his bottom again, but this time he barely registered the pain. He scrambled to his feet and started running away from the nightmare children. He could hear them shouting behind him, but he didn't glance over his shoulder to see if they were pursuing him. He fled across the street, not even checking for traffic, and at the far curb he stumbled over the broken pavement and fell face-first into a large pile of leaves.

He sank in for what felt like miles, totally submerged in the leaves. They were all around him, scratching at his face, blinding him. It was as if he were drowning in the dead leaves. He kicked and writhed...and then screamed again when he felt hands on his arms. He beat at whatever monster was trying to get hold of him.

"Billy, son, it's me! Calm down!"

The familiar voice registered, and Billy opened his eyes to see his father kneeling next to the pile of leaves, his arms held out. Billy leapt into those arms, wrapping his own around his father's neck.

"Billy boy, I'm so sorry," his father was saying, returning the tight hug. "I only let you out of my sight for a minute, and when I looked up again, I couldn't find you anywhere. Scared me to death. Please forgive me, I should never have been so neglectful."

"It's my fault, Daddy! I should never have wandered off."

His father pulled back, examining Billy with look and touch to make sure he was okay. "What happened to your mask and your trick-or-treat bag?"

"I guess I lost them."

"It doesn't matter. I promise, my phone is away for good tonight. We'll hit every house in town."

Billy looked around, finding himself back on the Jefferies Street he'd always known. There was the Haversham's fence, and the flamingos and gnomes in the Stevens' yard. Just down the road a bit he could see the oak with the tire swing hanging from one of its lower branches. Still, even though everything was once again familiar and well-lit, he sensed a darkness underneath it all, and the sound as a gust of wind sent the leaves stampeding across the pavement gave him chills.

"Can we just go home, Daddy?"

His father frowned at him. "Are you sure? I know how much you've been looking forward to tonight."

"I'm getting a little old for Halloween. Let's just go home, and maybe you can read me a story. Nothing scary though."

"Sure thing, Billy Boy," his father said with a smile, then he lifted Billy into his arms in a way he hadn't in years.

As he was carried home, Billy buried his face in his father's neck and tried to block out the sound of the autumn leaves.

IN THE ZONE

I've been a horror fan for almost as long as I can remember. That's not hyperbole either. One of my earliest memories is of my family watching the original airing of the 1979 TV adaption of *Salem's Lot*. I was five. I vividly remember certain scenes that have stayed with me for over forty years. That's power, and it was the power in horror storytelling that drew me to it more than any other genre.

I watched a lot of horror growing up. Slashers, Stephen King adaptions, anything I could catch on TV or save up the money to see at my hometown's one theater, the Capri. I took it all in, and it all influenced me as a storyteller.

But there was one thing above all others that had the greatest impact on me. *The Twilight Zone.*

Growing up in the 80s, I caught all the reruns of the original show and also devoured the 80s incarnation that adapted stories by so many horror greats. The show obsessed me, thrilled and delighted me, and it became a part of me in a way that only the things you love when you are young do. It also informed my idea of what horror is, of what horror could do. What struck me even at a young age was the surreal nature of the show, but also the subtlety. The world of *The Twilight Zone* was recognizably our world, but things would be just slightly off-kilter, enough to leave the viewer unsettled. The horror didn't come from things jumping out at you, but from *ideas*. Ideas that would linger and haunt the viewer long after the show was over. And of course, *The Twilight Zone* became famous for its trademark ironic twists.

All of this had a great influence on me when I first started writing. When I was around ten, I scribbled a series of one-page stories that were all *Twilight Zone* knockoffs. None of these survive today, but the one I remember most vividly for some reason was called "Laura or Horror?" Not exactly ground-breaking stuff, but it shows that from the very beginning I was trying to take the lessons *The Twilight Zone* taught me and use them in my own fiction.

And I'm still trying to do that even today. I think most of my readers can see that influence very strongly in my work, particularly my short fiction. Not that I'm trying to recreate the style or tone exactly, and I'm certainly not retelling the plots of episodes, but what I take from the show and implement in my work is a vibe, a sensibility, an idea of horror. My work is undeniably modern, and it often filters things through an LGBT+ lens, but I aim to create a recognizable world and introduce one or two surreal wrinkles into the mix, providing some twists along the way, that will linger in the reader's mind long after they have closed the book.

This collection I hope will stand as a testament to my love of *The Twilight Zone* and show the reader how I've transformed that love into my own art.

STORY NOTES

As a reader, I love when authors include story notes at the end of a collection. Just little behind-the-curtain tidbits about how the stories came to be, the spark of inspiration or some interesting information about each tale. Feel free to skip this if you so choose, but if you do read on, be warned. Herein lie spoilers, which is why I've saved it for the end.

"Turn the Lights Off on the Way Out" – This tale was written for one of the 2021 Cemetery Gates flash fiction challenges. The theme was "February Stars" and for some reason I instantly had the idea of an apocalypse where the stars simply started vanishing from the sky. My initial idea had to do with celebrities (metaphorical stars) gathering for a big party as they waited for the end of the world, but I got to thinking what I would do if I knew the world was about to end. And I would simply want to spend that time with my husband, so this gentle but heartfelt story was born.

"The Haunt" – Interestingly, this entire story was born from the first line. I can't say exactly where it came from, but I suddenly thought it would be cool to start a story by saying "Only two of the five survived..." but then never actually telling the reader which two. That was the initial conceit that led me to sit down and think up an entire story around it. Ghost stories are perhaps my favorite subgenre, so it felt natural to go in that direction.

"Reappearing Act" – This was originally inspired by an anthology call for stories that take the premises of the classic Universal monster movies and bring them into the modern era. I chose *The Invisible Man* but definitely put my own spin on it. I didn't make the anthology (they would only take one story for each premise), but I still think the story is exciting, at times amusing, but ultimately very disturbing.

"The Loophole" – This story was also born from my thought that at the end of the world I would want to be nowhere but with my husband. In "Turn the Lights Off on the Way Out" that manifested as something as sweet and tender, while here the story takes that premise somewhere a bit darker but still at its heart sweet. Originally I was calling this story "Til Death Do We Part" but when I got to the end, the new title revealed itself.

"The Shop of Lost Ideas" – This is one of a handful of really old, unpublished stories I included. To me, this one has a quintessentially *TZ* feel to it. I liked the notion of finding this strange little shop where you could buy ideas, inspirations, but in true *TZ* fashion, there has to be a price. There's always a price.

"In the Hands of An Angry God" – This is another story written for the Cemetery Gates challenge. If I remember correctly, the prompt had to do with an arctic setting of some kind, and the first thing that popped into my head for some reason was a snow globe. People trapped inside a snow globe, and what would that be like. I had a blast writing this one.

"Bird's Nest" – During the Covid lockdown, my husband started cutting our hair in the backyard. And honestly he continues to do so even now. During one of these trims, he looked at all the hair on the ground and told me that he'd read once that it was believed that if a bird took your hair and used it to build a nest, it would drive you insane. I found this a fascinating premise and instantly knew I had to weave it into a story like a strand of hair woven into a nest.

"The House of Mundane Horrors" – Another older one, and this one is almost pure humor. Every October I write Halloween-themed stories, so I have quite a few. With this one, I thought it would be fun to explore the holiday from the perspective of monsters. What would they do for fun, what would they find frightening?

"Campfire" – In my youth I wrote a lot of poetry, but as an adult I don't do quite so much. However, I do like to on occasion sit down and try my hand at it, almost always poetry of a narrative nature. Here I was following a prompt of a campfire story, but using the actual conceit of telling a story around the campfire and making that crucial to the twist at the end.

"Timing" – I love stories that deal with time. Time travel, time out of order, time anomalies. This story was inspired by the fact that my husband and I met later in life, and he always says he thinks we met at the exact perfect time because when he was younger he might not have been ready for this kind of relationship. So I got the idea of a character who gets the chance to go back in time, thinking he can use that to have even more years with his partner but finding that timing really is everything.

"In the Hands of an Indifferent God" – I also enjoy writing stories about writers and writing. Call that the Stephen King influence on my craft. As a writer, I know sometimes a story stalls and gets put aside, sometimes for a short period and sometimes indefinitely. I had a lot of fun exploring what that might be like from a character's point of view.

"Traveler's Rest" – This story was born from the title. Next to the town in which I live is a smaller town called Traveler's Rest. I've always been taken by that name, the peace that it suggests, so it was only natural that eventually I would turn that into a story.

"Future Tense" – More of my love of time travel. One thing that fascinates me about time travel is cause and effect. Usually it's how someone traveling into the past might inadvertently change the future, but here I wanted to look at how traveling to the future might actually create that future.

"Sestina for My Nightmare Man" – More poetry. I am a little obsessed with the sestina, which is a form of poetry with very rigid rules, the words that end each line of the first stanza having to repeat at the end of every line thereafter in a very specific pattern. It can be challenging to create a cohesive and coherent story while following the rules. Here I wanted to do something creepy and also make it rhyme, knowing that the rhyme scheme would change in each stanza.

"Strange Birds" – Call this my ode to Hitchcock. I liked the idea of taking the premise of *The Birds* but making it even stranger and more terrifying.

"Lost in the Wood" – Another story inspired by my husband. In the town in which we live, which is the town he grew up in, there is a mortuary called The Wood Mortuary. He told me he went there as a child for a relative's viewing, and his brother kept trying to dare him to go up the stairs to the second floor. He said he got halfway up the stairs before chickening out and running back down. I decided to extrapolate what he might have found if he'd gone all the way upstairs.

"If Heaven is a Library" – Well, this was born from my love of books and what I think my perfect Heaven would be ... and my most torturous hell. Originally I was going to have all the books be totally blank, but then I thought how much more exquisitely painful to let you get almost all the way through the story then never get the payoff.

"Two Boys at Summer Camp" – This one came from a prompt of summer camp horror. Having grown up on *Friday the 13th* and its endless sequels, the temptation was to go the slasher route, but then my mind started turning to the kind of camps that terrified me as a kid growing up gay in the 80s. This sweet little ghost story was the result.

"Heresy" – Sometimes in my fiction I like to create my own myths of creation and deities. That's what I did here, killing a god but then creating so many more.

"Sean Nichols Packs it Up" – I think most of us writers have had that experience where we wonder if it's all worth it, if anything will ever come of our writing, and some of us have even entertained the idea of giving it all up. I took that fear and insecurity and put it in a *TZ* set up to deliver a more uplifting ending.

"Unholy Ghost" – This came from a prompt for a ghost in a church or confessional. I decided not to go the literal route, and instead write a story that explores pain and trauma, but also culpability and the price one pays for keeping dark secrets.

"The Road of Many Hues" – This originally started as an idea for a poem, but then I had the notion to do little rhyming stanzas coupled with actual prose to flesh out a story of what is really valuable in life.

"Fifteen Minutes Fast" – Another of my older stories. This one is very straight-forward and probably of all the stories the one that most tries to recapture the feel of those *TZ* twists.

"Knowledge is Power" – Here I'm also trying to create my own myth, playing on Christian tales. One thing that always bothered me about the Garden of Eden was that God was trying to keep knowledge from Adam and Eve, and their punishment came about because they sought knowledge. For me, the pursuit of knowledge is the most important thing in life, so I wrote this story just to lead up to that last line.

"Brick at the Stonewall" – More time travel, and the devastating effects altering the past can have. I wrote this as part of a challenge to write complete stories at 300 words or less, and I sometimes find that kind of restriction thrilling.

"Horror Slasher Marathon" – Another of my Halloween stories, this one quite dark. Of course, this kind of violence is epidemic in this country, and from time to time I like to write stories that look at it head on and try to understand why. Not to condone the violence, but to try to figure out what we could do to curtail it.

"The Alien" – My last bit of poetry in the book, and not exactly a horror story but inspired by one. During the early months of Covid, writer Josh Malerman wrote a serialized novel called *Carpenter's Farm* and put it up for free on his website. He encouraged people to make their own art inspired by it, and I thought early on that the story in some ways could be a metaphor for growing up and growing apart from friends. This poem came from that.

"War on Christmas" – This was just a silly way to take the over-used phrase, "war on Christmas," and turn it into an absurd but entertaining story.

"Family Reunion" – Some stories of mine were written just for the twist and this is one of them. I like to do that kind of unexpected role reversal, where a character spends most of the story thinking he or she is one step ahead of another character only to have the tables turn and realized they were the patsy all along.

"The Tooth" – This is an old one, about grief and about moving on without completely letting go. I have written several stories that are born from my thinking that I don't know what I would do without my husband, and the way I deal with fears is often to put them in stories and explore them.

"In a Whirlwind of Autumn Leaves" – I decided to end this collection with a Halloween tale that I think is chilling but fun. Something else I like to explore in my fiction is the idea of alternate realities, different dimensions, and having someone pass from one to the other without at first realizing it.

And there you go, I hope you enjoyed these stories and that they will linger with you for a while. Until next time…

Made in the USA
Middletown, DE
23 May 2022

66102133R00102